cupcake cousins

Winter Wonders

by Kate Hannigan

illustrated by
Brooke Boynton Hughes

DISNEP • HYPERION
LOS ANGELES | NEW YORK

for my wacky & wonderful cousins in the nolan,
shea, and mcconville families
—k.h.
for kate hannigan, with admiration
—b.b.h.

Also by Kate Hannigan

Cupcake Cousins

Cupcake Cousins: Summer Showers

Text copyright © 2016 by Kate Hannigan
Illustrations copyright © 2016 by Brooke Boynton Hughes

First Edition, September 2016
10 9 8 7 6 5 4 3 2 1
FAC-020093-16204

Printed in the United States of America

Library of Congress Cataloging-in-Publication Data

Names: Hannigan, Kate, author.
Title: Winter wonders / by Kate Hannigan ; illustrated by Brooke Boynton Hughes.
Description: First edition. | Los Angeles ; New York : Disney-Hyperion, 2016.
| Series: Cupcake cousins; 3 | Summary: "Cousins Willow and Delia must
save the day when a blizzard threatens to ruin Cat and Mr. Henry's wedding
in the third book in the illustrated Cupcake Cousins series"—Provided by publisher.
Identifiers: LCCN 2016009267| ISBN 9781484716632 (hardback) | ISBN 1484716639 (hardcover)
Subjects: | CYAC: Baking—Fiction. | Blizzards—Fiction. | Weddings—Fiction.
| Christmas—Fiction. | Cousins—Fiction. | Family Life—Michigan—Fiction. | Michigan, Lake—Fiction. |
BISAC: JUVENILE FICTION / Social Issues / Friendship. | JUVENILE FICTION / Cooking & Food.
| JUVENILE FICTION / Holidays & Celebrations / Christmas & Advent.
Classification: LCC PZ7.H198158 Win 2016 | DDC [Fic]— dc23
LC record available at https://lccn.loc.gov/2016009267

ISBN 978-1-4847-1663-2
Reinforced binding
Visit www.DisneyBooks.com

Publisher's Note: The recipes contained in this book are to be followed exactly as written, under adult supervision.
The Publisher is not responsible for your specific health or allergy needs that may require medical supervision.
The Publisher is not responsible for any adverse reactions to the recipes contained in this book.

SUSTAINABLE FORESTRY INITIATIVE | Certified Sourcing
www.sfiprogram.org
SFI-00993

THIS LABEL APPLIES TO TEXT STOCK

Contents

Catherine Sutherland
& Henry Rickles

invite you to join them in
a merry celebration of love & joy,
good food & good friends
for their wedding!

Christmas Day, December 25th
at high noon

at Whispering Pines Bed & Breakfast
in Saugatuck, Michigan

the wedding party

flower babies

June Bumpus-Baxter
July Bumpus-Baxter
August Bumpus-Baxter

junior bridesmaids

Delia Dees
Willow Sweeney

best boy

Sweet William Sweeney

musical accompaniment

Darlene Dees
Violet Sweeney

The Reverend Roland Rickles Presiding

Chapter 1
in a winter wonderland

Y ou girls look colder than icicles on an igloo!"
came Cat Sutherland's voice from the yellow
porch of the Arts & Eats Café. Willow Sweeney and
her cousin Delia Dees had been making snow angels
and playing hide-and-seek among the Christmas
decorations in the front yard.

Now they were in the middle of a snowball fight.
And Willow's throw proved pretty good as she
pelted Delia squarely in the chest. Delia was ducking
behind a bright red sleigh for protection, taking aim
to launch a snowball right back at her cousin, when
Willow called over to Cat.

"Come join us!" she shouted. "You can help build a snow fort!"

"And then we'll launch an attack on the rest of the family," added Delia, though she hurled one last snowball at Willow for good measure.

"Why don't y'all join me in the kitchen? I'm fixin' to make some snowball cookies, and I'd be happy to pour hot chocolates."

As much as Willow loved snowball fights, snowball cookies and cocoa sounded a lot more tempting. Delia seemed to agree, and they raced to meet Cat on the porch steps. Together the three crunched through the frozen snow toward Whispering Pines next door.

"I'm so happy you're here again, Willow," Delia said as they stepped through the door into the warm kitchen. "Cat and I have been counting down the days until the Chicago families arrived."

Willow had been counting too. "I couldn't wait to come back to Saugatuck," she said, shaking the snow from her springy hair, "even if it is freezing this time of year."

"I wish you lived here with us," said Delia with a big grin. "You make everything more fun! Especially Christmas!"

"And weddings too, y'all," reminded Cat. "We've only got a few days."

Willow peeled off her mittens and began blowing on her freezing hands. As Cat and Delia wriggled out of their layers of scarves and hats and heavy sweaters, Willow stepped farther into the kitchen. Her eyes drank in the familiar sights: the white curtains at the windows, the island counter in the middle of it all, the pots and pans hanging from the rack just above the island.

Willow let out a deep sigh. Saugatuck was just what she needed right now.

After everything that had gone on at school these past few weeks, Willow finally felt her shoulders relax. Spending winter break with Delia in Cat's kitchen, well . . . there was no better place on earth. Willow closed her eyes and made a quick wish that she could leave Chicago behind and live here all year long.

"Nice holiday touch," she said, poking the mistletoe bunches that dangled from red ribbons between the pots and pans. "Everything looks so cheery for your Christmas wedding, Cat!"

"I'm so grateful y'all are going to be my junior bridesmaids," Cat replied. She was pouring milk into a chocolate mixture on the stove.

Delia gave Willow's arm a playful nudge, and Willow nudged her right back. Nothing could beat being junior bridesmaids together. And their dresses were so much better than the pink disasters they'd worn at Aunt Rosie's wedding. This time, Cat had allowed them to pick the color: a dark green, and made of soft velvet too.

Just thinking about Cat's wedding and her first Christmas in Saugatuck, Willow felt as if her whole body were bouncing—from her hair all the way to her toes. Though at this time of year, she was wearing thick wool socks instead of flip-flops.

"And I'm thankful y'all are willing to help me bake everything for my wedding day," Cat said, stirring the cocoa with a long wooden spoon.

Willow stopped her bouncing. "You'll be in the kitchen with us, right? Over the summer, you promised to share your cooking secrets. Will you still? Because I could sure use them."

"I never go back on my word, y'all," Cat began. "So here's the first secret: hot cocoa tastes best when it's made nice and slow on the stove, with a dash of salt and vanilla."

"Salt?" gasped Delia with a grin. "Don't you mean sugar? You know how bad it can get when those two are mixed up!"

Willow smacked her hand to her forehead. The

memory of their salty lemonade made her cringe. That was back during Aunt Rosie's wedding, when the cousins first met Cat.

"We've got no time for mix-ups this week, y'all," Cat said seriously. "The wedding is on Sunday, and only the three of us will be making the food. I don't want to bring in any strangers—not when I have you two girls."

And Cat gave them both a confident wink.

Delia winked back, but Willow didn't feel so confident. She was remembering all the cooking they'd done on their summer vacations. Willow and Delia had saved Aunt Rosie's wedding cake, and they'd pulled off the baby shower without a hitch. Well, maybe there were one or two hitches. . . . But this time, the stakes felt higher. It was Cat after all, a real-live chef! And Mr. Henry was the owner of Whispering Pines. Even though they both felt like family, Willow knew deep down this was different. Could she and Delia really cook for something as important as Cat and Mr. Henry's wedding?

Without any disasters?

Willow shot a look over at her cousin, who was beaming like a Christmas tree strung with lights. So Willow forced a grin too and tried to imagine what sort of things she, Delia, and Cat would make together this week. Maybe with advice from a professional like Cat, plus a little Christmas good luck—if she could find any—everything would turn out okay.

"I thought I'd put you girls in charge of the wedding desserts," Cat said. "Think that's something you two can handle?"

And with Cat's Southern way of talking, it came out sounding like *hayn-del*.

Delia nodded, her braids springing in all directions, almost like Willow's crazy curls. "Of course we can! What will you do while Willow and I are handling desserts?"

"Y'all, some people dream of climbing mountains or inventing new gadgets," Cat explained as she poured the cocoa into three mugs. "For me, it's making my own weddin' cake. I'll be busy as popcorn on a skillet these next few days. So I'm really counting on you girls."

Delia promised Cat that her wedding desserts were in good hands. And raising their cocoa delicately in the air, the three chefs clinked mugs.

Willow inhaled the warm, chocolatey smell and avoided Delia's gaze. She just wasn't feeling the same confidence, not after all that had happened at school last month.

"Maybe you could call in a few caterers to help out," Willow said softly, shrugging her shoulders. "Just in case we mess up or something."

Delia stopped sipping and stared over her mug at Willow. She raised a single eyebrow, questioning. But Willow stepped away, as if to say, *Later. Not now.*

She planned to explain it all to Delia at some point. But with Cat sitting here, it wasn't the right time.

Thankfully the door from the porch opened, and Willow's little brother, Sweet William, thumped into the kitchen. He was wearing his heavy snow boots, and Bernice, the family's enormous Bernese mountain dog, was following closely on his heels. The honking at the screen door let them know Gossie and her three goslings, Bill, Pat, and Jimmy, were nearby.

"I need some carrots and maybe some celery, please, Ms. Cat," Sweet William was saying, his cheeks nearly as red as his wool hat. "Bernice and Gossie and me are making reindeer feeders. I got some string from Mr. Henry, 'cause we're going to hang the treats from the trees. If I can catch Santa's reindeer, maybe I can ask him for a special Christmas present!"

Cat grabbed a small basket and began filling it with treats that could tempt reindeer: celery, carrots, a few red apples, and green pears. "Don't hang things all in one place," she advised. "Spread it out through the whole yard."

Bernice let out a happy bark and wagged her tail, and Sweet William gave a quick salute. Then they marched back onto the porch with Gossie and her army of goslings waddling close behind.

"I wonder what he'll do with Santa if he catches him," Cat said, the screen door making a muffled *thwack!* "Maybe take a ride in his sleigh?"

"He doesn't really need that," Delia said. "My mom and dad found an old-fashioned sleigh at a flea market and parked it out front of the café. It looks just like something Santa would drive."

"Didn't I hit that thing with a snowball?" wondered Willow, tipping the cocoa mug to drink up the last precious drop. "Maybe Santa left the sleigh here years ago when he built a new one. We'll have to tell Sweet William about it."

Cocoa cups emptied, Cat pulled out the ingredients to make the snowball cookies. She led the cousins in mixing and mashing and rolling and baking, calling them real professionals. Willow pulled out her tattered recipe notebook from the polka-dotted bag she'd left near the door. And as Cat shared her wisdom, Willow took detailed notes of every step.

"Sifting the flour and sugar gets the bugs out," Cat explained from behind a cloud of powdery sugar, "and it gets the lumps, too."

With the cousins busy forming the cookie dough into small balls, Cat began working on the batter for her wedding cake. And she shared a few more baking secrets—"eggs should be room temperature," "butter should be soft"—as she whisked. In between sifting and stirring and mixing, Willow jotted down every word.

Before long, the kitchen was filled with the mouthwatering aroma of freshly baked cookies. When the timer beeped, Delia and Willow pulled the two trays out of the oven and set them on the stovetop to cool.

Willow inhaled the delicious smells, then let out a deep sigh of relief. "Phew! They're not burnt!"

Again, Delia raised a single eyebrow in Willow's direction, silently asking a question.

"It smells so good in here, I hate to leave," Cat

announced. "But I'm all out of flour, girls, so I have to run to the store." Tugging her cat's-eye glasses from her nose, she took a moment to clean them with the corner of a tea towel.

"I know this kitchen is safe with y'all in charge. I'll be back, quick as a snowman on ice skates." And she slipped into her coat and hat without bothering to take off her flour-dusted apron.

With the kitchen to themselves now, Delia and Willow rolled the warm cookies in powdered sugar. Then they began lining up their treats in a container to keep until Cat's wedding on Sunday.

"Willow," Delia began softly, "what is going on? You're usually the one who's crazy for doing all the cooking. But now you want Cat to call in backup chefs in case we mess up. What's the matter?"

Willow slowly rolled another snowball cookie through the powdered sugar. She didn't know where to begin. She fidgeted in her socks, sneaking a peek at her cousin's worried face.

"School," Willow said, finding it hard to get the

words out. "We had a bake sale last month. I made dozens of cupcakes and cookies. But it turns out they weren't very—"

Willow caught her breath, blinking fast so the tears wouldn't come. Cupcakes weren't something to cry about. She sniffled once, noticing how quiet the kitchen had become. Delia was standing motionless as she waited for Willow to go on. But what more was there to say?

"Delia, everybody laughed at me."

Cat's Nice-'N'-Slow Hot Cocoa

Make this delicious wintery drink when the temperature starts to dip.
But as with whipping up lemonade in the summertime, be sure you
don't confuse the salt and the sugar!

Ingredients:

8 ounces dark or bittersweet
chocolate
1 teaspoon vanilla

4 teaspoons powdered sugar
1/8 teaspoon salt
4 cups milk

Directions:

1. Make sure you have an adult's help.

2. Break the chocolate into smaller pieces using your hand or a dull
knife.

3. Add the chocolate, vanilla, powdered sugar, and salt into a pot on the
stove. Over low temperature, stir until the chocolate has melted and all
the ingredients are mixed together.

4. Pour milk into the pot, and bring to a simmer.

5. Heat thoroughly, about 5 minutes. Take turns stirring with your
cousin or friend so the milk doesn't burn and your arm doesn't fall off.

6. Pour into mugs, and enjoy!

Makes 4 mugs of hot cocoa.

Chapter 2
needing some christmas magic

I t's okay, Willow," Delia began, sitting down on the stool beside Willow. "Everybody messes up now and then. It doesn't matter."

"Yes, it does, Delia." Willow's words were low and quiet, all the spring gone from her voice. "It's one thing to mess up here, when it's just family. They have to love us anyway. But at school, well . . . you know how it can be."

Delia gave Willow's sugary hand a squeeze. It told Willow that she *did* know.

"You just need to get your confidence back," Delia said, nibbling a snowball cookie, then sharing it with

Willow. "Since it's winter, there aren't any humming-birds to bring us good luck. But maybe we'll find a little Christmas magic instead.

"At Christmas, Willow," she added, her voice growing cheerful again, "anything is possible! Everybody knows that!"

Ding-dong!

At the sound of the doorbell, Delia grabbed Willow's hand again and dashed out of the kitchen. They zoomed through the swinging door, around the big dining room table, and raced for the front door to see who was there. But Grandma and Grandpa Bumpus beat them to it. They were holding the door open for a stranger in an old-fashioned top hat to step inside from the cold.

"If it's all right, I'd like to talk on the porch," the man said. "That way I can keep an eye on my horse."

Horse? Willow scrambled over to the window next to the front door for a peek, Delia right beside her. They both pressed their noses to the cold glass to get a better look at the tall black mare.

"I adore horse-drawn carriage rides," Grandma was saying. "And as we said on the phone, we'd like your carriage service to be our gift to Cat and Mr. Henry for their wedding."

Grandpa pointed toward the pine trees, explaining where the carriage could park on the wedding day. "But we'll need to keep this quiet until then so that it's a surprise." And turning to his granddaughters in the doorway, Grandpa said, "Think Grandma can make like a chrysanthemum?"

Delia and Willow shrugged, knowing Grandpa was always ready with a flower joke.

"She'll have to stay *mum*!"

Willow couldn't help but laugh. Stepping out onto

the porch to get a closer look at the beautiful horse, she told them their wedding gift was a great idea. "I think Cat and Mr. Henry will love it!"

"And it's really creative," Delia added with a pout. Then she heaved a frustrated sigh and folded her arms into an X.

Willow knew exactly why.

She and Delia still didn't have a wedding gift to give Cat and Mr. Henry.

"By the look of things, everybody in the whole family is coming up with great ideas," Delia complained in a cranky whisper. "If we don't decide soon, all the good ones will be taken!"

Delia was right. Uncle Delvan and Aunt Deenie were giving one of his paintings. Delia had said it featured pickles and lemons, two of Mr. Henry and Cat's favorite things. And Willow's parents were giving them cookbooks full of pickling recipes.

Willow tugged on Delia's arm and dragged her back into the dining room to talk.

"Our gift can be just as good as Grandma and

Grandpa's," she said, placing her hands on Delia's shoulders so they squared off face-to-face. "We just have to agree on something."

"We've agreed that it has to be special," Delia said, a hint of huffiness in her voice. "But that's where our agreeing ends. Can't you just say yes to putting our savings together? So we can buy Cat and Mr. Henry something really special?"

Willow shook her head. "Delia, it would be more special if we put our *talents* together and *made* them something special! Like me with karate and you with, with . . ."

"With helping animals? Or people? I don't think so, Willow."

Even though cooking was something they were good at—or *used to be* good at, Willow reminded herself—it wasn't anything she was willing to do now. Willow searched her brain to come up with other ideas.

"It's funny," Delia said, pressing her forehead to Willow's, their matching amber eyes just inches apart.

"We usually look at things the same way. But now, you and I can't seem to see eye to eye on this one."

Just then, their big sisters flitted into the dining room, both a little breathless.

"Have you seen the ukuleles?" asked Willow's sister, Violet. "We need them—and fast."

"We've just come up with something really special for Cat and Mr. Henry's wedding present," gushed Darlene, who was Delia's big sister. "But you'll have to wait to find out what it is."

"They're going to be so happy," Violet bragged, and Darlene nodded in agreement. "Our playing was pretty much the best part of Aunt Rosie's baby shower in the summer, don't you think?"

Willow thought a lot of things just then. But since Santa Claus could be listening, she knew she probably shouldn't speak a single one of them.

"We're going to be rehearsing a lot now," Darlene said as she and Violet headed for the staircase, "so you two need to help Aunt Rosie with the triplets. We told her we'd do it, but now we're too busy."

"That's right. And Willow, you can't go off and hide like you've been doing in Chicago," Violet called as she reached the second floor. "You've got to do stuff again! Help with the babies, get back in the kitchen, that kind of thing!"

Get back in the kitchen?

Willow scowled.

And help with June, July, and August?

Willow wrinkled her nose, clearly disgusted by the thought. While she loved Aunt Rosie and Uncle Jonathan, and she loved the *idea* of her newest cousins, babies were a handful. Willow always came away from her visits with the triplets smelling like sour milk and wearing mysterious gunk in her hair and on her clothes. Even her best pair of sneakers was stained with baby gunk!

Delia tugged on Willow's arm, leading the way back into the kitchen. As the heavy door let out a *whoosh* behind them, she turned to Willow and handed her another cookie.

"Listen, cousin. Right now you're a little bit Grinch mixed with a whole lot of Scrooge. I'm going to work on the Christmas magic. But you've got to help me! Now let's figure this out: What can we do for Cat and Mr. Henry?"

Chapter 3
what's orange and goopy and goes "splat"?

It was early evening when Willow and Delia finished hanging Christmas lights around Whispering Pines with Mr. Henry. They'd been able to agree on helping with decorations, but they still could *not* agree on a gift.

The sky was a purply-blue color as the sun set over the water, but Willow didn't need a clock to tell her what time it was. Her rumbling stomach made it clear that dinner should be served. And fast!

"Girls, I'm so glad to see you," chimed their aunt Rosie as Delia and Willow stepped into the kitchen. Aunt Rosie was their moms' younger sister, and she used to look like she belonged in downtown Chicago: her clothes were stylish, her shoes were pointy. But these days, since she was dealing with her and Uncle Jonathan's new triplets, Aunt Rosie was a little rumpled.

"Your big sisters are busy with a wedding surprise," Aunt Rosie said. "But they were sweet to tell me that you girls could handle dinnertime. Thank you so much for helping!"

"Helping?" began Willow.

But before any more words escaped her lips, something orange and creamy smacked onto her cheek. *Splat!*

Delia saw it hit and burst out laughing.

"Don't worry, Willow! It's just a little—" And as Delia reached over and patted her cousin, more orange goop shot through the air. It splattered onto Delia's arm in two places—*Splat! Splat!*—as well as onto the refrigerator, a white cabinet, and a few of the dangling pots and pans.

A shrill cheer went up, and both cousins turned to see who the offending gloop flingers were.

The triplets were lined up in their high chairs, smiling and cooing and smearing their mushy orange dinners on their trays. Not to mention their faces, Willow noted, and their ears, hair, even toes.

"June, July, and August are just starting their dinners, girls," began Aunt Deenie as she wiped a bit of gunk off her own nose. "Sweet potatoes and carrots."

"It's so nice of you to take over the feeding," added

Willow's mom, who was running a paper towel over a pencil she'd plucked from her hair. "Just watch Baby June. She's a little dangerous with that spoon."

And as if on cue, curly-haired June flicked her baby spoon, sending another glob of the goopy mush into the air. It landed on Aunt Rosie's exhausted face.

"I really appreciate the help, girls," their aunt sighed. She ran a finger across her forehead, then licked it clean. "Your moms and I are going to take a little rest by the fireplace in the front room. You're real dears."

And like a burst of wind off Lake Michigan, they blew out of the room, the heavy door swishing behind them.

"Wait a minute!" protested Willow. "How did we get put in charge of these babies? We're just kids! Is this legal? Are we even old enough to feed babies?"

Delia couldn't seem to stop herself from laughing. Taking a seat on one of the stools, she told Willow it couldn't be too hard. After all the things Willow had pulled from Bernice's mouth, was this so bad?

Splat! A bit more goop landed on the counter between them.

"Besides," Delia said, wiping it up with a towel, "one of the best things about wintertime is having snowball fights. At the rate the triplets are going, they're going to be great!"

Willow tilted her head to one side, studying Baby June. She watched her chubby little arm pull back, back, back. Then the fling.

Splat! This time, the orange glop smacked against the oven door, all the way on the other side of the kitchen.

"You know, you're right, Delia! These three will make great snowball fighters one of these days. With them on our team, we'll definitely beat our big sisters! We can make it a holiday tradition!"

Delia grinned and spooned a bit of gloopy dinner into Baby August's mouth. He kicked his feet happily.

"That's the right spirit, Willow. Christmas magic! We'll teach the triplets all our traditions. And tomorrow we'll come back in the kitchen, and we'll make something yummy for Cat's wedding."

Willow scooped a glob of the orange dinner and fed Baby July another bite. She felt a smile start to glow deep inside. There might be something to Delia's "Christmas magic" after all.

"And when we're done with that, Willow, we can go into town and buy a wedding gift. See, everything's coming together!"

Buy a wedding gift?

Willow didn't have any money to buy gifts! "Delia, we've got to *make* them something. Mr. Henry *makes* Cat's vegetables into a delicious sauce! And they *make* their own pickles—these guys love homemade stuff! Can't we just grab some of Sweet William's modeling clay and a few sticks from the yard? And *make* them a sculpture?"

"A sculpture?" gasped Delia. "No way! Are you serious?"

Splat!

Now all three of the babies were laughing and kicking their feet as Willow wiped orange food off her eyebrows. There seemed to be quite a few things keeping her and Delia from seeing eye to eye.

Chapter 4
to help, or not to help

It was bright and early-ish the next morning when Delia and Willow climbed out of their beds. Pulling blue jeans over long-john pajamas and tugging thick sweaters over their heads, they dressed for the day. Then both cousins raced down the staircase in search of Mr. Henry's brother, Reverend Roland Rickles. With the reverend's help, Delia was going to show Willow one of her favorite things to do in Saugatuck.

"You'll love helping out at the food pantry," Delia explained a little breathlessly. "If you lived here with me, we could go together all the time. Everybody there is really nice."

Willow's eyes lit up. That sounded much better than having to go back to Chicago and her school there. "I'll ask my parents, Delia. I want to move here so badly!"

As they pushed open the door into the kitchen, their eyes fell on three bowls of fresh goop waiting on three clean high-chair trays. This time the goop was pale red instead of orange, and it smelled like strawberries.

"Girls, you did such a good job feeding the triplets yesterday," said Aunt Rosie with a tired grin. She was trying to slip a squirming Baby July into one of the high chairs.

"We thought you could help with this morning's breakfast as well," said Willow's mom, her eyes running down one of her daily checklists as Baby June wriggled in her arms.

"We would really love to help, Aunt Aggie," Delia began. She pulled an extra pencil from her aunt's bun and handed it to her in a helpful gesture. "But we're already really busy."

"Right," added Willow, the grinchy scowl back on her face. "Really busy."

Just then, the door swung open, and Violet and Darlene shuffled in, still wearing their pajamas. They looked sleepy as they carried their ukuleles.

"But look who's here to help!" said Willow. She threw an arm around each of the sisters' shoulders and gave them both a peppy squeeze. "Violet and Darlene would love to feed the triplets for you."

Darlene shook her head. "No we wouldn't! We've got to rehearse our song!"

Delia gave a cheerful wave good-bye and backed across the kitchen floor toward the door. "Sorry, we've got to run!"

Violet let out a huff, wanting to know why Willow and Delia were getting out of triplet duty.

"Reverend Rickles is waiting for us—we're help-ing out at the food pantry," explained Willow as she rushed to Delia's side.

"Helping at the food pantry?" asked Violet, her voice softening. She reached out to catch Willow's sleeve as she hurried by. "Willow, that's the perfect way for you to face your problem. Why don't you bake something for them?"

But Willow didn't slow down. This was not a con-versation she was ready to have—especially not with her big sister.

"Bye-bye! Have fun with the triplets!" Delia sang as they rushed out the door and into the yard.

The cousins zipped their coats as they ran for Reverend Rickles's truck. Climbing into the backseat amid a flurry of excited hellos and good mornings, Willow felt a little stab of guilt for what they were leaving behind. Aunt Rosie had looked exhausted, her eyes puffy and her voice scratchy from lack of sleep.

While the triplets were cute, they were a lot of work. "Maybe we should go back to the Whispering

Pines kitchen," she whispered, "and help out Aunt Rosie."

"You're right, she does need help," Delia said, each of her words puffing into the cold air. "But the food pantry needs our help too. There are a lot of hungry people who need a hand."

Willow stared out at the pine trees in the yard, feeling a little confused. "Sometimes it's hard to know the right thing to do. Especially when there's more than one *right thing*!"

Finally, Reverend Rickles backed the cranky old truck down the driveway. And in moments, the wheels were crunching over the frozen snow and heading toward downtown Saugatuck.

"Willow, your cousin here has been our star volunteer this year," Reverend Rickles said, adjusting his rearview mirror so he could see the two cousins better in the backseat. "She bags groceries for people who need it, plays with the children who could use a friendly face. I hear her say that everybody at the food pantry is nice. But good gravy! From our per-spective, *she's* the nice one."

Delia picked at her mittens, clearly embarrassed by Reverend Rickles's praise. But Willow loved learning about all the things Delia was doing in Saugatuck. It made Willow want to move here even more.

"How many people do you think will come for your pancake breakfast this Christmas?" Willow asked, leaning forward in her seat so Reverend Rickles could hear her over the road noise. The old truck was big and boxy, and the tires made a noisy thrumming sound that filled the backseat.

"Last year, we fed around eighty hungry souls," he called over his shoulder. "We call it our Christmas miracle—somehow we always manage. But this year, I'm a little worried. We're expecting more than a hundred people. Things are tight all over, so a free meal really helps out."

More than a hundred people to feed? That sounded like a lot of work. "How can you even do that?"

"Well . . ." Delia began. And her eyebrows knit together as she worked through the numbers. "We could have six volunteers make twenty pancakes each. Or maybe we have ten volunteers make twelve pancakes. . . ." Delia went round and round with different possibilities until finally she shrugged and gave Willow a grin. "The pancake breakfast might need a little Christmas magic too."

Practically shouting over the noise, Reverend Rickles told Willow how volunteers made all sorts of home-cooked dishes to share throughout Christmas Day. "We start with pancakes in the morning, and then we spend the whole afternoon feasting. It's great. And everyone who helps out, well, I consider them to be Santa's helpers. They have a way of making everybody so happy."

Delia said they even had a Santa Claus come through and hand out presents to little kids. Then dropping her voice to a serious tone, she added, "It's not the real one, you know. Last year, it was Chester Bacon, the newspaper editor, dressed up in a red suit and white beard. I'm not sure who they'll ask to play Santa Claus this year."

The road noise died down as they pulled up to the redbrick storefront. Delia wiped at the moisture on the glass beside her, and Willow leaned closer to peer out the truck window. The words LAKE MICHIGAN FOOD PANTRY were painted in gold lettering across the wide storefront window. White holiday lights framed the entry, and a sign taped on the door said EVERYONE WELCOME.

Willow was curious and excited as she and Delia piled out of Reverend Rickles's truck. They filled their arms with boxes of paper plates, tablecloths, and plastic forks.

"If I lived here with you, Delia, I'd help out at the food pantry too," she said with a bounce. A bag of paper napkins slipped from her pile of boxes, and Delia caught it before it hit the ground. "Maybe we should forget about cooking for Cat's wedding. Instead, we could help here and serve the Christmas breakfast. This sounds like a special place."

Delia nodded, fumbling with her own stack of boxes. "I hope we can figure out a way to do both, Willow. Help with the Christmas breakfast here *and* the Christmas wedding back at Whispering Pines."

Willow turned an idea around in her head. Maybe Violet was right. Maybe she should try to get over the bake-sale disaster by making something for the food pantry. But when would she find time for that?

"There are still a couple more days. We'll think of other ways to pitch in," she said, trying to convince herself as much as Delia.

Reverend Rickles held a door open with his foot as the cousins stepped into the food pantry's dining area. His arms were loaded down too. As they carried in their supplies for the Christmas breakfast, four or five volunteers rushed over to take their heavy boxes.

"Give those here," said a friendly woman wearing a bright red sweatshirt. "You look as if your arms might fall off!"

"Thanks, Mrs. Rudolph," Delia said. And she introduced Willow all around.

Willow nodded and gave a little wave to each volunteer. But she had to bite her lip to keep from laughing. And that's because every one of them—from the short man on the left who was no bigger than Sweet William to the tough-looking woman on the right who seemed like she belonged in a motor-cycle gang—was wearing the same red sweatshirt as Mrs. Rudolph.

In white letters across the front was printed: SANTA'S ELVES.

"Delia and her cousin are here to help," began Reverend Rickles. "I figured we could begin by setting up the chairs and tables for the pancake breakfast."

As everyone mobilized to get the tables in order, Willow saw a flash of orange scurry past.

"What was that? It nearly tripped me!"

"That's just Tabitha," Delia said as she dusted off a few folding chairs. "She's a tabby cat who adopted the food pantry. Nobody knows where she came from or where she goes all day. She just stops by for a meal now and then. Like everybody else!"

Chapter 5
just the right gift

Before long Reverend Rickles's truck was back at Whispering Pines, and the cousins climbed out with hearty good-byes and promises to help again before the pancake breakfast on Christmas Day. Reverend Rickles told them not to worry.

"You two will be so busy getting my brother's wedding ready, you won't have time for pancakes," he said. "And, hey, the breakfast is our Christmas miracle, right? We'll get everyone fed, one way or another! When it's done, I'll race over here to Whispering Pines and meet the bride and groom as they walk down the aisle."

The cousins waved good-bye, then decided to pop into the Arts & Eats Café. Before getting back to Cat's kitchen next door, Willow and Delia were eager for warm mugs of the café's famous apple cider. And besides, at the café they could figure out plans for a wedding present without Cat nearby to overhear.

If they could just agree on something.

"I've been thinking," Delia began, leaning forward and letting the cider's steam warm her face. "I know you're avoiding the idea of making more food for people, after the bake-sale incident and all.

So what if we bought them matching sun hats? You know how Mr. Henry has that straw one. What if we got him a fresh hat, and Cat one exactly like it?"

Willow closed her eyes, wrapping her hands around the warm mug and breathing in the scents of apple and cinnamon. "Thanks for understanding, Delia. But sun hats? Does that mean you don't like my sculpture idea? I can't believe you don't agree that our gift should be homemade."

"We don't have the right materials to make a decent sculpture. What about buying them matching beach towels? And we could sew letters on them! One could say *His* and the other *Hers*!"

Willow shook her head. Matching beach towels and sun hats were for summertime, she reminded Delia. They should agree on a present that Cat and Mr. Henry could use now.

"Like thick socks. Or warm scarves! You know how to knit, don't you, Delia? I can knit a rectangle, but nothing more complicated than that."

Suddenly, Delia got very quiet, staring off toward

the lake like she was deep in thought. And Willow recognized that look right away. She could almost see the wheels turning in her cousin's head. Delia Dees had an idea.

"Maybe, Willow," she began softly, "we need to think bigger. Like what our big sisters are doing. You're still taking violin lessons, right? And I play the flute in my school's orchestra. I think we should play a mushy love song as our gift to Cat and Mr. Henry! And the flute and violin are way more classy than the ukulele!"

Willow nearly spilled her mug of cider as she got to her feet. "That's a great idea, Delia! We should have thought of this earlier. We'll wow them with our musical talents!"

The cousins slurped down what was left of their hot ciders and grabbed their coats. They were in a hurry to get back over to Whispering Pines and catch up on the wedding desserts. The sooner they finished the next treat, the sooner they could rehearse their mushy love song!

"We're supposed to make the peppermint bark now," Willow said excitedly. "You can do the mixing while I write down Cat's secrets. Maybe if I memorize all her tips, it will keep me from messing up again."

Both cousins tugged on their wool hats and their thick mittens as they ran out the café door and across the freezing yard toward Whispering Pines. Hearing the wind whipping through the trees, Willow zipped her coat as high as it would go.

"Don't be so hard on yourself," Delia said, the

blustery wind carrying her words. "Do you remember Aunt Rosie's wedding? When I was so worried about everything being perfect? You taught me this, Willow: We have to at least try. Think of all the fun we'll miss out on if we don't!"

It was a few hours later when they trudged back through the yard to the Arts & Eats kitchen, their wool hats and scarves smelling like peppermint and chocolate. Twinkly lights lined the roof and both the front and back porches of the café, and they shone brightly against the backdrop of white snow in the early-evening darkness. Willow breathed deeply and felt her nostrils freeze from the cold air.

Delia was just finishing off a bit of the peppermint bark that Cat had given them as they left—Cat's way of saying thanks for a hard day's work in the dessert factory over at Whispering Pines. "Between the bark and the sugar cookies, the chocolate-dipped pretzels and the cheesecake squares, y'all kept as busy as a pair of robins on nesting day."

Once they'd peeled out of their wintery layers, Willow plopped down at a table in the empty café and wrestled with her heavy boots. She couldn't help but giggle at Delia, who was so eager to start practicing their mushy love song for Cat and Mr. Henry that she kept hopping from one booted foot to the other like a nervous flamingo.

"Why don't we write them a love song?" she began. "What rhymes with *Henry*? Or better yet, what rhymes with *Saugatuck*?"

Willow thought for a few moments. *"Woodchuck? Potluck? Dump truck?* This doesn't sound too romantic, Delia."

They stared into each other's faces for a beat or two. Then they agreed to perform a mushy love song they already knew rather than write a whole new one.

"I'll run upstairs and get my flute," Delia said, finally slipping out of her snowy shoes. "Where's your violin? In your car? Your suitcase?"

Uh-oh.

"It's back in Chicago," groaned Willow. "I didn't

want to practice it over winter break. Does your dad have one? Or your mom?"

Delia shook her head and sat down beside Willow, looking dejected. She was quiet for a while.

"We've both got to give a little bit, Willow, or we're never going to get a present ready in time for Sunday's wedding."

Willow knew Delia was right. But what could they possibly do in just a few days? It was already Thursday afternoon! The sun would be setting soon!

"I think you're right," Delia began. "Maybe homemade is exactly what we should be doing. So I'll forget about going shopping."

Willow sat up straighter in her chair, thrilled that Delia had finally come around to her way of thinking.

"But let's face it, Willow, we shouldn't be trying to make a homemade sculpture or homemade His and Hers beach towels or homemade knit socks and scarves. Or even a homemade mushy love song. We don't want to copy our big sisters—they're already going to sing for Cat and Mr. Henry. That's *their* thing.

"What we should be doing is making homemade food. That's *our* thing, Willow! That's what we're good at!"

Cat's Famous Peppermint Bark with Bite!

The secret to this holiday favorite is easy to spot: Chocolate! In two colors!

Ingredients:

2 4-ounce semisweet chocolate bars

½ teaspoon peppermint extract

2 4-ounce white chocolate bars

4 peppermint candy canes

Directions:

1. Make sure you have an adult's help.

2. Line the bottom and sides of a 9 x 9–inch square baking pan with parchment paper or tinfoil.

3. Break up the semisweet chocolate bars into smaller chunks. Place chunks in a microwave-safe bowl and melt for about 40 seconds. Be careful not to burn the chocolate! Stir with a spoon for a few seconds before heating again, about 20 more seconds. Keep heating and stirring until the chocolate is smooth and melted.

4. Once the chocolate is melted, add ¼ teaspoon peppermint extract and stir.

5. Pour the chocolate into the lined baking pan. Use a spatula to spread it out smoothly. Then refrigerate the pan until the chocolate has set, about 10 minutes.

6. Follow the same steps to melt the white chocolate. Break up the white chocolate bars into smaller chunks. Place the chunks in a microwave-safe bowl and melt for about 40 seconds. Again, be very careful not to burn the white chocolate. Stir with a spoon for a few seconds before heating again, about 20 seconds. Repeat until the white chocolate is smooth and melted.

7. Add ¼ teaspoon peppermint extract to the white chocolate and stir.

8. Pull the pan from the refrigerator, and pour the white chocolate over the dark. Use a clean spatula to spread out the white chocolate layer smoothly.

9. Place the peppermint candy canes in a plastic baggie, and seal it. Use a rolling pin to hammer the baggie, breaking up the candy canes into smaller bits.

10. Sprinkle the candy cane bits onto the top layer of the chocolate.

11. Refrigerate the pan until the chocolate has completely hardened, about 20 minutes.

12. Pull the pan from the refrigerator, and break up the peppermint bark into pieces with your hands or cut the bark into squares with a dull knife (and an adult's help!).

Makes about 8 servings.

Chapter 6
fancy food

Willow didn't want to admit it, but Delia was right. The best gift they could give Cat and Mr. Henry was something they made themselves.

In a kitchen.

At a stove.

Together.

"Okay, I'll do it," she finally announced. "And you promise that nobody's going to laugh at us?"

"Willow, what exactly happened at the bake sale? Can you tell me?"

Willow looked around the café at Uncle Delvan's paintings. She didn't know where to begin. "I baked for over a week to get ready for it. Cookies, cupcakes, everything. I worked so hard. But I guess some of the things I made started to turn bad."

Delia gasped. She leaned in closer to hear what came next.

"The cookies were stale by the time the kids bought them. So they began throwing them like Frisbees. And the cupcakes, I don't even want to tell you about them. Some kids, well . . . they spit them out! And then it all became a big joke."

Delia shook her head, promising Willow it wouldn't be like that again.

"That was a fluke, Willow, a one-time mistake. But I know you, and you're really good in the kitchen. So you've got to pick up your whisk and get cooking again. Like right now!"

Willow brightened just a bit. With her cousin beside her, maybe she could forget the bake sale ever happened. "We're in this together, right?"

Delia nodded, and she bounced in her thick socks the way Willow was always doing. Her braids sprang this way and that, like Willow's crazy curls, as she crossed her heart.

Willow couldn't stop the smile from taking over her face. "Finally, we're agreeing! We'll make Cat and Mr. Henry an amazing dessert!"

"You mean dinner," corrected Delia.

"Dessert," Willow insisted. "Who doesn't love dessert?"

"Dinner," said Delia, her voice rising. "Dinners are fancy, Willow. Dinners are romantic. A fancy romantic dinner is the perfect wedding present!"

Willow let out a long sigh. Even when they were agreeing, they still weren't seeing eye to eye.

"Okay, Delia, why don't we do both—a fancy dinner *and* a fancy dessert?"

Delia began bouncing again, her fuzzy socks sliding on the slick wooden floor. She danced around the table in a very un-Delia sort of way. Willow couldn't keep herself from laughing. And she jumped to her feet beside her cousin, and together they slipped and

slid across the floor in their winter socks, like they were skating on a frozen pond.

Right away, Delia was ready to get started. She began making plans for the fanciest, most romantic dinner she could think of. Willow, on the other hand, was no help. She didn't know the first thing about cooking a romantic dinner. When her mom and dad wanted a fancy meal, they went out to a fancy restaurant—without Willow, Violet, or Sweet William.

"Fancy dinners have things like lobster and caviar," declared Delia, taking a seat at the table beside Willow again. "And other things, like fancy potatoes, fancy butter, fancy rolls. We should write this down, Willow!"

Willow wasn't so sure about fancy food. She'd heard of caviar before; it was fish eggs, wasn't it? Willow forced a smile, trying hard not to look like a grinch again. She decided to let Delia be in charge of all the dinner plans. So as Willow's mom passed by, pencil sticking out of her hair and checklist tucked in her back pocket, Willow figured it was time to place a grocery order.

She called her mom to the table, asking Delia to explain her plan for making the fanciest, most delicious, most amazing dinner of Cat and Mr. Henry's lives.

"Lobster?" asked Aunt Deenie, slipping into the chair beside Willow's mom. Her eyebrows shot up in surprise. "Are you girls sure about that? Lobster is fancy and all, but really? You don't want to just make pizza or something?"

"We're sure," Delia said confidently. "What's the fanciest kind of meal Uncle Liam writes about in his restaurant reviews for the newspaper? I'm betting it's lobster, lobster, lobster!"

Aunt Deenie told them that Uncle Delvan knew a thing or two about cooking seafood.

"And your dad knows a thing or two about eating it," added Willow's mom with a grin. Her pencil made a scratching sound on her notebook as she started another list. "We'll get them to help you girls out. We have to run to the grocery store anyway. So we'll meet you here in the café in a few hours, once it's closed for the night."

"Right," said Aunt Deenie, the surprise still on her face. "You girls can try out your lobster dinner tonight and see if you like it."

Willow and Delia were in a heated game of crazy eights when they heard the door open and felt the rush of cold air from outside.

"Who's ready for some fancy cooking?" called

Willow's dad, his cheeks pink from the wintery night. He and Uncle Delvan were lugging a cooler between them. And Aunt Deenie and Willow's mom weren't far behind, bags of groceries in their arms. Willow thought her parents looked happy with Aunt Deenie and Uncle Delvan, as if they were right at home in Saugatuck.

"Wouldn't it be great if we lived here all year long, just like Delia and everybody?" she asked, giving her mom and dad a peppy grin as she shut the door behind them. "We could make fancy dinners like this all the time! What do you think? Is it time to wave bye-bye to Chicago?"

Willow's mom said something about facing fears and getting back on saddles, sounding a lot like Violet and Delia. But she was interrupted by the lobster project.

"The first step, girls, is to find the biggest pot in the cabinet and fill it with water," directed Uncle Delvan, easing the cooler onto the floor in the middle of the kitchen. "Then put the pot on a burner and bring it to a rolling boil."

Willow's mom had her coat off now and began running her pencil down a checklist. With each item she ticked off, Aunt Deenie pulled it from the canvas bags to show the cousins.

"Potatoes? Check!"

"Heavy cream? Check!"

"Garlic? Check!"

"Lobsters?"

At that, the dads flipped open the lid on the ice cooler and pulled out two snapping, squirming, wriggling lobsters. "Check!" their fathers called.

Willow let out a howl of surprise. "Hey, they're still alive!"

"What are you doing, Dad?" hollered Delia, covering her head. "Put them back!"

Just like the snapping lobsters, the cousins began doing their own squirming and wriggling too. They pressed themselves as far away from the cooler and the creepy crawlers as they could possibly get.

"What's the matter?" said Uncle Delvan. "Are you surprised to see the lobsters still clicking their claws?"

"They're supposed to be alive before we cook them," Willow's dad explained. "Then when the pot is nice and hot, we drop them into the boiling water. *Mmm!* Delicious."

Willow was so grossed out by the idea, she plugged her fingers into her ears and began to sing, *"La la laaaa!"* She turned away and stared hard into Delia's face, not wanting to risk seeing the wriggling lobsters again.

Delia, on the other hand, seemed to be outraged. And she couldn't pull her eyes away. Willow eventually stopped her song and peeked over her shoulder to see where Delia was staring. Another few lobsters had clawed their way out of the cooler, flopping right onto the kitchen floor.

"I can't do this," Delia said, clambering up onto the countertop. "No way, I can't. I'm officially declaring myself a vegetarian. That's it. From now on! I'm not eating anything that can crawl around on its own!"

"I thought you already were a vegetarian," piped up Sweet William, who had just rounded the corner with Bernice, Gossie, and the feathered triplets, Bill, Pat, and Jimmy. "Or are you a *veterinarian*? I always mix those up."

"She *wants* to be one of those, and she just declared herself to be the other," said Willow, who was scrambling onto the countertop to join her. "Delia can't boil lobsters for both those reasons."

The cousins pulled their knees to their chests to keep the runaway lobsters from snapping their toes or making off with their thick socks. Willow tried hard not to screech while her dad and Uncle Delvan chased down the lobsters to put them back into the cooler. It was like a seafood rodeo!

Bernice let out a woof

and jumped toward the creepy, crawling creatures. But a few snaps of a lobster's claw near her black nose made Bernice rethink that decision. The geese began to honk, as if they disapproved of the lobsters' snapping.

"Maybe we should just make a salad," Willow suggested. A shudder rattled her shoulders as she stared at the lobsters splayed across the kitchen floor. "With the right vegetables, salad can be extra fancy."

Delia groaned, dropping her head onto Willow's shoulder. "Extra fancy was what I wanted," she said. "But Willow, this was a little too fancy!"

Chapter 7
seeing red

The cousins were up and out the door early Friday morning, bundled up for a walk along the lakeshore and confident they would find no lobsters out there waiting for them. Delia had been explaining all about how the waves froze along the water's edge like carved statues. Willow wanted to see for herself.

But just as their boots hit the porch, a voice called out behind them from deep inside the house. "Where are you two going?"

And then another to match. "Hiding away while everyone else does all the work, I suppose?"

The voices belonged to their big sisters. Willow

and Delia turned to face them, the icy wind off the lake whipping through the back door of the Arts & Eats Café and into the gallery. Willow hoped it didn't blow any of Uncle Delvan's paintings off the wall.

"We're doing plenty of work," snapped Delia, and she gave her scarf a defiant toss over her shoulder.

"That's right," agreed Willow. And she tossed her own scarf over her shoulder, like Delia. But the wind knocked it right back off. It was hard to look tough in blustery weather. "We're helping Cat with the wedding. So you two can stop bothering us. We're busy!"

"Busy? All you two ever do is goof off," said Darlene with a scowl. "You're having a snowball fight or going off with Reverend Rickles into town or eating cookies—"

"While Darlene and I are working so hard to get our present perfect for Sunday's wedding!" interrupted Violet. "Willow, what's the deal? Have you made something for the food pantry? Or done anything? You can't just give up when things get hard, you know. I didn't give up when swimming got harder. That's how I won all those medals."

Willow felt her shoulders tense up. She didn't want to hear about Violet's medals. She didn't want to think about the kids at school laughing at her bake-sale disaster. She wanted to handle this her own way, with Delia.

"Just leave us alone, Violet, please," she called into the wind, her words coming out a little harsher than she'd meant them to be. "I'm doing things, okay?"

The cousins turned back toward the lake, marching angrily down the Arts & Eats Café's back steps and into the yard. Having a big family was one thing, but having big sisters was something else entirely.

"They're so bossy," complained Delia.

"They're so annoying," added Willow.

"And they're so wrong!" they both shouted at the same time.

Willow and Delia trudged across the frozen layer of snow toward Whispering Pines and the bluff there. The enormous tree in the middle of Delia's yard looked cold, and the blueberry bushes seemed in need of winter coats. Their bare branches shivered in the wind.

"Let's forget about our sisters for a while," Delia said with an encouraging smile. She threw her arm around Willow's shoulders. "We'll be busy in the kitchen the rest of the day, and we can make time to do something special for the food pantry. But for now, I want you to see what I love about winter here!"

Willow was surprised how much she liked being outside, even though the temperature was so cold that she couldn't feel her nose. Back in Chicago, she was always hurrying away from winter. But here it felt different.

"There is a lot to explore," Delia said, slipping the cord to her binoculars around her neck. "The hummingbirds are gone to Mexico at this time of year, but I've seen snowy owls and white rabbits. There are all sorts of winter animals and birds to show you."

"You have your own binoculars?" exclaimed

Willow, a touch of awe in her voice. Delia carried her own first-aid kit too. Sometimes, Willow thought to herself, it was as if her cousin were a Girl Scout leader. Or a secret agent. "The only reason to have binoculars in the city is for spying on neighbors in tall apartment buildings. Do you actually use them here?"

"Of course," said Delia with a laugh. She lifted them to her eyes and focused on a cluster of trees near the water's edge. "How else are you supposed to spot hawks? Like this one!" And she passed the binoculars to Willow, who quickly pressed them to her own eyes.

"I can't believe it," Willow whispered. "You can

see everything with these!" And as she turned and pointed the binoculars out toward the water, Delia let out a choking gasp.

"First let me take them off," she croaked. "Still . . . connected!"

"Sorry!" Willow exclaimed, helping her cousin unloop the cord from around her neck. "I got a little excited. But there's so much to see!"

Delia told Willow to stay put and enjoy the binoculars. She needed to run into the kitchen at Whispering Pines and pick up her mittens. "I think I left them there yesterday. It's too cold to walk along the beach without them. I'll be right back."

As Delia headed for the kitchen, Willow put the binoculars up to her eyes again and looked out to the water. She felt like a pirate queen at sea.

Turning her gaze toward the shoreline, she scanned the treetops in search of more birds. Then she rotated her body like a light in a lighthouse, slowly turning, her binoculars taking in the trees up the coast. But as the binoculars caught the yard and

Whispering Pines, Willow jumped. Instead of birds on branches in the far-off distance, suddenly close-up images of the porch furniture filled her vision.

"That must be Grandma's chair," she mumbled to herself. "And that's the spigot for the hose along the side of the house—probably the one Sweet William used on Aunt Rosie's baby shower last summer. And that's . . . What is that?"

Willow held her breath, trying to keep the binoculars steady. What was she looking at? The color red filled her field of vision. And was that a bit of white? A bright red hat with a round white pom-pom at the tip?

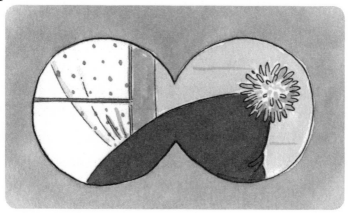

Willow pulled the binoculars from her eyes and glanced down the pathway that ran along the side of Whispering Pines, her eyes adjusting. But the yard was empty of color, only the browns and tans of fallen leaves and bare tree trunks amid an inch or so of snow.

Where had that red come from?

Willow put the binoculars back up to her eyes and scanned the whole yard now. But the red was gone. All she saw was a close-up view of crinkly bark, white snow, and wintery brown leaves.

Thwack!

The door let her know that Delia was finished in the kitchen.

"Willow! You're not going to believe this!"

Delia rushed down the porch steps, tugging her mittens onto her hands. Her cheeks were flushed, probably from excitement as much as from the cold.

"It's the peppermint bark!" Delia began, trying to keep her voice to a whisper. "The squares we made yesterday! At least a dozen, maybe more, are missing!"

"What?" Willow whisper-shouted back. "How can that be?"

"And the other treats—the snowball cookies we made with Cat, and the sugar cookies and pretzels and cheesecake squares—are gone too! Somebody took off with at least half the desserts!"

Willow shook her head back and forth like she couldn't believe her ears. Who would do such a thing?

"And when I asked the uncles about it, you won't believe what they told me," Delia said, her breath leaving white puffs in the air. "They just shrugged and said maybe Santa's elves took them!"

"Santa's elves?" exclaimed Willow. And she pulled the binoculars to her eyes again, looking deep into the empty yard that connected Whispering Pines and Delia's yellow house next door. She was hoping to catch a glimpse of red again. "Elves? You don't really think . . . well . . . Could it be?"

Delia sounded baffled. "I believe in Christmas magic, but elves? Really, Willow? *Elves?*"

Chapter 8
on the trail of treat thieves

after a long walk along the frozen beach, where Willow got to see and touch the frozen waves for herself, the cousins climbed the steep bluff staircase back up to Whispering Pines. They'd agreed not to mention elves or missing desserts to Cat.

"But we'll have to get cooking as soon as we can," Delia said, her eyebrows pointed like knitting needles and her voice determined. "We'll replace whatever treats have gone missing."

"Cat's got high hopes for this wedding," Willow said, a bit of worry creeping into her voice. "We can't let any kitchen disasters ruin it."

And like a parade, the memories of their kitchen disasters marched through her mind: the salty lemonade, the splattered smoothie, the dog-eaten treats for Rosie's wedding shower. And then there were the lemon cake, lemon cookies, and lemon bars they'd destroyed in search of the missing family heirloom that Grandma had given Delia.

"Maybe we should borrow your mom's notepad and start a list of all the things we don't want to go wrong at Cat's wedding," Delia said with a sigh. "No exploding blenders. No splattering mixers. No cookies catching on fire. No salty sweets. And most important, no disappearing desserts!"

Willow stomped her boots, trying to warm her toes. Who would take their wedding treats? Sweet William and the geese? The uncles? The big sisters? And how could they possibly find the time to bake more desserts to replace the ones that had disappeared?

"And the missing desserts aren't all!" Willow said, a bit of panic rising in her voice as she thought more about Christmas morning. "We still have to make a wedding gift for Cat and Mr. Henry. And then there's the pancake breakfast at the food pantry to think about too!"

"We can do it, Willow. We just have to believe we can," Delia said calmly, her mitten running over the snow-covered railing. "Christmas is all about giving and sharing and doing good. We'll figure out a way to make more wedding desserts, cook up a great wedding present, and help out at the food pantry."

Willow wondered whether they should just forget about Cat's wedding and put all their energy into the food pantry. But Delia wouldn't hear of it.

"You said it before," Delia declared, her snowy hands on her hips. "Sometimes it's hard to know the right thing to do. Especially when there's more than one right thing!"

"But the food pantry needs us," began Willow, "to set the tables and serve the food. . . ."

"Sure, but Cat needs us too. She's counting on us, Willow." Delia paused, reaching her hand over to her cousin's shoulder. "I know you're afraid of another disaster. That people are going to laugh at us, the way they laughed at you at school. But we can't quit. We can do this, all of it!"

They were back at Whispering Pines now, piling their many layers of winter coats and boots and mittens and hats in the dining room. Suddenly, a strange sound caught their attention. It was gurgling. No, maybe creaking? Willow lifted her head to hear better, her eyes shooting toward the front of the house. Delia was at her side in seconds, her hand clutching Willow's arm.

"Maybe that's the dessert thief," Willow whispered, pressing in close to her cousin. "We've got to catch him in the act! Or her!"

"Let's get them," Delia whispered back with a nod. "Do your karate thing!"

"I don't have a karate thing," Willow confessed. "We never attack real people!"

"Well, I don't have an attack either," Delia replied in a loud whisper. "I just have the first-aid kit to take care of someone if *they* get attacked!"

After shushing each other, the cousins quietly slunk along the dining room wall until they reached the hallway. Willow could still hear the shuffling sounds on the hardwood floor and an occasional squeaky floorboard. She clutched Delia's arm tighter. Silently, they counted to three, their fingers in the air. Then they pounced into the hallway.

"*Aha!* We've got you!" Willow shouted, her arms and legs thrust out in a karate stance.

"Surrender the snacks!" called Delia, tucking in just a little bit behind her cousin. "Or else . . ."

At the sound of their voices, a cry went up. But it wasn't the cry of bandits being caught or dessert thieves confessing. It was the cry of a baby being woken up.

"*Shhhhhh!*" scolded Willow's mom. "You're waking Baby August!"

"Delia," hissed Aunt Deenie, who was holding curly-haired Baby June and pacing back and forth, "we're just getting the triplets off for their naps. What are you thinking, making such a racket?"

"If you girls don't mind keeping it down," said Aunt Rosie, who was trying to be sweet but was clearly exhausted as she patted Baby July's back. Aunt Rosie looked like she could use a nap too. "The babies like to be walked a bit before they fall asleep. In fact, your big sisters were supposed to help us with this. I wonder if you girls—"

Willow and Delia quickly whispered their apologies as the three aunts and the three babies circled past on their sleepy-time route.

"We're busy in the kitchen today," Willow said. And again she felt a stab of guilt for avoiding triplet duty. She shot a quick look at Delia, her eyes questioning. "But I guess we can help a little. What if we sang them a few Christmas carols?"

Aunt Rosie seemed overjoyed.

"We can do the quiet ones," Delia suggested, "not the *fa-la-la-la-la* ones."

And the three aunts pressed in closer, gently rocking the three babies in their arms.

But just as they agreed on a song, Delia raised her hand.

"I'm sorry to interrupt. And singing together like this will make a great tradition," she whispered a little frantically. "But did you happen to see anyone going in or out of the kitchen this morning? Any strange or suspicious characters?"

"We need to solve a sort of mystery," added Willow, forgetting her quiet voice, "that's going on with the dess—"

"*Shhhhh!*" came the response from all three aunts. "The babies!"

"But the desserts!" whispered Delia and Willow together.

"We didn't see anyone *suspicious*," said Aunt Deenie, rocking sleepy Baby June. "But there are plenty of *strange* characters in this family!" And she laughed at her own joke.

"I've only noticed family coming and going," whispered Aunt Rosie, her hand gently stroking Baby July's tiny head. "Nothing unusual."

"Honestly, Willow, we haven't seen anyone near your desserts in that kitchen," her mom added quietly, one hand covering Baby August's ear so he wouldn't stir back up. "The only thing I can tell you is that maybe Santa's elves were here. Now let's start singing and get these babies to sleep!"

This Recipe Is for the Birds!

Sweet William's birdseed treats make a great gift for the feathered friends in your life. Just look for the right branches for hanging the pinecones, and you can create a special kind of Christmas tree.

Ingredients:

String or twine
10 pinecones
1 cup creamy peanut butter
2 cups birdseed

½ cup cornmeal
Parchment paper
Cookie sheet

Directions:

1. Make sure you have an adult's help.

2. Cut the string or twine into 10 24-inch strips. Tie one string to the top of each pinecone, knotting it securely. Leave even lengths of string on each side of the knot. This is how you'll hang your ornaments.

3. In a bowl, mix the peanut butter, birdseed, and cornmeal together to form a paste.

4. Using your fingers, mash the mixture onto the pinecone and into each of its layers.

5. Have a cookie sheet nearby with a sheet of parchment paper spread on top to save on cleanup. When you finish with each pinecone, set it on the cookie sheet.

6. Take your tray of pinecones outside, and tie each pinecone to a sturdy branch. Decorate the branches with popcorn garlands too, and you'll have a holiday tree that's for the birds.

Makes 10 pinecone ornaments.

Chapter 9
a burning desire for bananas

After a few rounds of "Silent Night," "Away in a Manger," and all the other quiet Christmas carols they could think of, Willow and Delia tiptoed back into the kitchen. The babies were asleep, and the three aunts looked as if they could nap too.

The cousins discovered Grandma and Grandpa seated on the kitchen stools, pouring cups of coffee and talking about the horse-drawn carriage they ordered for the wedding.

Grandma wanted to go out on a ride. "Just to test it out. Don't you think that's a good idea, girls?"

But Grandpa teased that she just wanted to get

him alone. "She's a dangerous romantic," he told Willow and Delia, tapping at the green-and-red mistletoe clippings that dangled on ribbons from the pots-and-pans rack above them. "Sometimes I call her Miss LeToe, the way she's always hanging about trying to steal a kiss!"

Delia told them about the fancy food she and Willow were planning. "Only it's not going so great."

Willow pointed out that she hadn't gotten her turn yet. She and Delia needed to hurry up and get cooking, or they wouldn't have even a plate of crumbs to give Cat and Mr. Henry.

Just then, the door to the porch opened, and more family trudged in from the yard. First came Willow's dad, along with Uncle Delvan and Uncle Jonathan. Sweet William, Bernice, and Gossie with her goslings trailed behind them.

"We were hoping to find all of you here," began Willow's dad, setting an enormous pot of popcorn onto the countertop. "Sweet William has been setting out snacks for Santa's reindeer. And he's very interested in decorating the biggest pine tree in the yard with Christmas treats for the birds and other animals."

Setting another popcorn pot beside the first one, Uncle Delvan said they needed everybody to help out. And balancing a third big pot on the edge of the counter, Uncle Jonathan pulled off the lid and revealed what was inside: even more popcorn.

"We could use some extra hands stringing this popcorn into garlands to decorate the tree," Willow's dad said. "Anyone here good with a needle and thread?"

Grandma said she loved the idea, and she patted the stool beside her for Uncle Jonathan to take a seat. Since Uncle Jonathan was a kindergarten teacher, everybody knew he was great with crafts. Together they threaded their needles and began poking them through the fluffy popcorn.

Uncle Delvan pulled a bag of bird-seed from his coat pocket, and Willow's dad pulled a jar of peanut butter from his. They showed Sweet William how to make bird-seed Christmas ornaments to hang on the branches along with the popcorn garlands. Grandpa sipped his coffee and said he was ready if anyone needed him.

"Sorry, Sweet William," Willow said, "but Delia and I have a lot to do in the kitchen today. So if you don't need us, we'll start cooking!"

Willow and Delia moved over to the stove, a little bounce in both their steps.

"I've made a decision, Delia. This is the fanciest dessert I can think of." And Willow gulped, barely able to get the words out amid her excitement. "I want to make Amazing Flaming Bananas Foster!"

"Flaming?" asked Delia, the bounce coming to an abrupt stop.

Willow ignored her. "It seems easy enough, not too many ingredients. But the *wow* comes when we set it on fire! That will really impress Cat and Mr. Henry, don't you think?"

Delia's eyebrows shot to the ceiling. "Flaming?" she said again, this time a little louder. And she quickly began shaking her head.

"Yes, Delia! A dessert that's on fire! What is more special than that? We'll go down in history! People everywhere will ask us to make desserts for their weddings once they hear about our flaming bananas!"

Delia folded her arms across her chest like a big X. "Nope. No way. No go."

Willow couldn't believe her ears. What *wasn't* there to love about this dessert idea?

"What's the matter?" she asked. "Is it because you can't stand bananas?"

Delia threw her hands in the air, looking at Willow as if she were the one with flames shooting off her.

"Are you crazy, Willow? I thought you meant *fried* bananas, not *on fire* bananas! Don't you remember what happened last summer? When the fire trucks came because of Darlene and Violet's burning cookies?"

Willow tried to assure Delia that the fire department wouldn't be called out over their Amazing Flaming Bananas Foster. She promised they'd be extra safe, extra cautious. And their dessert would be extra delicious.

But Delia wouldn't budge.

"I couldn't help but overhear," began Uncle Jonathan, shyly approaching the cousins at the stove. "It sounds like you're talking about making bananas Foster."

When Delia and Willow nodded, Uncle Jonathan went on.

"I had a job one summer at a hotel. And bananas Foster happened to be our specialty. I'm pretty good at it, if you want some help."

Willow bounced in her fuzzy wool socks and threw her arms around their uncle. Jonathan was just what she needed to convince Delia that this was the best wedding present ever! In the history of wedding presents!

"Do you hear this, Delia? They make bananas Foster at hotels. Fancy hotels! This is a fantastic idea!"

"A fantastic idea," Delia said, "is to make something with icing—as in *ice*-ing, the opposite of *fire*!"

But Willow plunged ahead. She sliced the bananas and arranged them in the pan with butter, cinnamon, and the other ingredients. Then, when it came time to light the match, she looked up to find everyone in the kitchen staring.

"This is it!" she cheered, trying to sound convincing. "This is the big moment! When we do this for

Cat and Mr. Henry, they'll remember it their whole lives!"

And as Uncle Jonathan struck a match, the pan lit up in flames. Fire danced across the bananas! Orange and blue fingers of flame climbed higher and higher from the stovetop!

"Whoa, I should move this away from the burner," Uncle Jonathan said, his voice sounding a little worried. And he stepped away from the stove, balancing the burning pan away from himself as the flames rose.

Suddenly, everyone at the island in the middle of the kitchen jumped backward, scraping the wooden stools across the floor as they scattered away. "Give him room!" shouted Uncle Delvan, and he protectively pulled Sweet William behind him.

"Look at that fire!" shouted Willow, clapping and bouncing. "It's incredible! How can you not want to make this, Delia?"

Uncle Jonathan let out another "*Whoa!*" and tried to find a place to put the flaming pan, which clearly was growing heavy in his hand. He set it on the marble counter at the island, catching his breath as he did.

And catching something else as well.

One of Cat's mistletoe decorations, which was festively dangling from the pots and pans like a Christmas tree ornament, was now on fire! Its green leaves and red ribbon were engulfed in flames, a burning ball of holiday cheer!

"Put it out!" shouted Willow, looking around for a glass of water or anything to douse the dangerous decoration. "Stop that fire!"

Delia grabbed the mug of Grandpa's coffee and splashed it at the flaming mistletoe. It was a direct hit, and immediately the flame went out. At the same time, Uncle Jonathan slipped a silver lid onto the flaming pan, snuffing out the burning bananas.

"Phew! That was exciting!" hollered Sweet William, clutching Bernice with one hand and Uncle Delvan with the other. "That made my heart kick a beat!"

"I think you mean *skip* a beat," Delia corrected. "Not *kick*."

"No, I mean *kick*," Sweet William said. "Because that's exactly what Cat's going to do when she sees you made another disaster in her kitchen. She's going to kick you right out!"

Fried-but-Not-Flaming Bananas

Here is an easier, less dangerous version of bananas Foster. Top ice cream with the warm, gooey bananas for a delicious treat. And without the flames, it meets with Delia's approval!

Ingredients:

2 tablespoons butter
2 bananas, sliced lengthwise
½ cup brown sugar
½ teaspoon cinnamon

1 teaspoon vanilla
1 pinch salt
2 scoops ice cream (Willow prefers vanilla)

Directions:

1. Make sure you have an adult's help.

2. Melt butter in a pan over medium heat.

3. Add the bananas to the pan. Let them cook for about 3 minutes. Then flip them and cook another 2 minutes.

4. Mix together brown sugar, cinnamon, vanilla, and salt. Pour mixture into the pan.

5. Reduce the heat to a simmer. Cook for about 2 more minutes.

6. Scoop ice cream into a bowl. Spread the bananas and sauce over the ice cream.

7. Do not even think of setting fire to your dessert or your kitchen! "Nope. No way. No go," says Delia.

8. Eat the warm bananas with the ice cream, and enjoy!

Makes 2 servings.

Chapter 10
another great gift idea

It stinks in here! What did you do?"

Thwack! Thwack!

Willow looked toward the kitchen door and saw
Violet and Darlene standing there, their faces wrinkled
up like dried apples. Darlene was pinching her nose.

"Oh, no, Willow," said Violet. "Not again!"

"Cat is not going to like it if you burned her wedding desserts," Darlene said, her voice sounding
nasally as she switched from pinching with her left
hand to her right. "Or has she already fired you?"

"We're doing just fine," Willow said, trying not to
sound annoyed.

And she sampled a bit of the fried bananas. Her dessert tasted good, despite setting part of Cat's kitchen ablaze! She held her spoon out toward Delia, encouraging her to take a bite. But Delia just blinked at Willow a few times, sealing her lips into a tight line. She wasn't going to give in on this one.

Willow felt her shoulders begin to droop again. Violet was right; this was another disaster to add to her long list of them. She dropped the pan into the sink with a noisy clatter as Violet and Darlene started their bragging.

"We're not sure what's been going on here," Violet said with a wave of her hand. "But we've been working on Cat and Mr. Henry's wedding present. They're going to love it!"

"You're probably dying to know, so we'll tell you. It's a song we wrote ourselves," Darlene announced. "Both the music and the lyrics!"

As the rest of the family *ooh*ed and *aah*ed over their big sisters, Willow and Delia started cleaning up their mess.

"Great," Willow said, giving the banana pan an extra-hard scrubbing. "The wedding is a day away! And they're going to give the best gift of all, while we're going to have nothing."

"Don't worry, Willow, we'll come up with something good," Delia said, her voice sounding encouraging. But Willow's hopes were fading fast. She and Delia had finally agreed on an idea, but

both the fancy lobster dinner and the fancy flaming banana dessert had turned into disasters.

And from the sound of things, it was getting harder and harder to beat what the rest of the family was doing. How could she and Delia make something better than a song? Or a carriage ride? Or an oil painting with pickles?

"At this rate, even Bernice will have a better gift than us," Willow complained. "No offense intended, Bernice."

Bernice wagged her tail, looking as if none were taken.

"Come along, girls," called Willow's dad from the doorway. "We're all going out to string the popcorn garland in the pine trees and hang up the birdseed decorations. This is Sweet William's present to Cat and Mr. Henry. He needs our help to pull it off."

Christmas for the birds and furry animals?

Willow couldn't help but groan. Delia dropped her spatula into the sink.

"His gift is perfect!" said Delia, her voice dripping with frustration.

"No kidding," grumbled Willow as she pulled a tea towel over her head. "The only thing wrong with it is that *we* didn't think of it first!"

Chapter 11
the wedding countdown begins

Saturday morning arrived bright and cheery, with a pink sky in the east and a dusting of snow on the windowpanes that reminded Willow of powdered sugar.

"Merry Christmas Eve!" called Delia from her bed, which she had somehow already finished making for the day. "I heard a rumbling in the driveway, and it sounded just like Reverend Rickles's old truck. Let's get downstairs before he leaves. We can catch another ride to the food pantry!"

Willow threw off her covers and tugged on a fresh sweater. Sure, there were more wedding desserts to make and presents to bake, but the food pantry needed them too. And if today was Christmas Eve, Willow realized, tomorrow was the pancake breakfast! Tomorrow, as in just twenty-four little hours away!

"Good gravy! I'd love to have you girls help again," Reverend Rickles said as he opened the door on his truck. "We're planning to do a bit more decorating, make the place look festive. By any chance do you know how to cut paper into snowflakes? That sort of thing?"

Willow and Delia jumped into the backseat, assuring Reverend Rickles they were expert decorators. The truck smelled of warm bread, and Willow's mouth began to water as she thought about breakfast.

"Help yourselves to a cranberry muffin," Reverend Rickles said, nodding toward a basket beside him. "Picked those up at a farm down the road. I stopped here hoping to get some of Cat's cinnamon rolls, but I couldn't find her."

When the cousins arrived at the food pantry,

volunteers in red sweatshirts were busy putting up a Christmas tree in the dining hall.

"Hi, Mrs. Rudolph," said Delia with a friendly wave. "My cousin Willow and I are here to help again."

"Wonderful, girls! That's so nice of you," she said. "Some of the helpers are over there, bagging up holiday treats to send home with families. But we could use you girls over here. How are you with scissors and glitter glue? Could you help us make the place look a bit more cheerful?"

After a busy morning spent cutting and gluing for the next day's pancake breakfast, the cousins headed back to the kitchen at Whispering Pines. Willow had big plans for her second try at making the wedding present, describing the wonders of a chocolate soufflé.

Only she sounded just like Cat with her Southern twang whenever she said it: *su-FLAY!*

Delia was explaining the beauty of a fancy fish stew, only she couldn't remember how to pronounce it.

"It sounds like *bull-ya-base*, I think," she tried as they trudged through the snowy yard. "Or *boil-ye-bwoss*? Oh, Willow! Do you think we should be making dishes that we can't even pronounce?"

Willow stopped in her tracks, her hair whipping in the cold wind off Lake Michigan.

"Hey, I thought you were a vegetarian now," she said. "Why are you thinking about making a stew out of fish?"

Delia said there was a big difference this time. "First of all, the fish won't still be alive and flopping around on the kitchen floor. And second, I'm not going to eat it myself. It would be for Cat and Mr. Henry!"

Willow pointed out that they already had the ingredients for chocolate soufflé—chocolate, eggs, butter, sugar—but not for the fancy fish stew. Delia, however, wasn't even close to surrendering. "Your bananas Foster idea went up in flames," she told Willow confidently. "Now it's my turn to get a fancy dinner right!"

Their voices were just starting to get heated when they walked into the warm kitchen. Cat and Mr. Henry were perched on the wooden stools and sipping mugs of cocoa. So the cousins quickly dropped their discussion about extra-special, extra-delicious, extra-amazing wedding gifts.

"Howdy, y'all," Cat said with a smile that was brighter than a flashlight. Willow had heard of brides being radiant around their wedding day, but Cat was like sunshine itself. And Mr. Henry was beaming too, his cheeks pink like a summer sunburn. Willow couldn't help but smile right back. "How are my chefs today?" Cat asked in a singsong voice. "Ready for more bakin'?"

And with Cat's Southern way of speaking, it came out sounding like Bernice's favorite treat, *bacon*.

Immediately, Willow was reminded of Aunt Rosie's wedding shower, when Bernice devoured Cat's bacon treats and fruit tart. She cringed at the memory. Cat had been so angry then. Now here they were baking for Cat's wedding! If she found out that half her wedding treats had vanished, she would be even more furious. She was certain to blame Willow and Delia for the disappearing desserts.

"We're ready," Willow said with a nervous gulp.

"Ms. Catherine and I were just discussing tomorrow's wedding," said Mr. Henry. He took another sip of his cocoa as he peered over at the cousins. When he set his mug down, Willow noticed a small chocolatey mustache over his upper lip.

"Oh, that's right," Delia said in a worried voice. And she began tugging on her braids. "By this time tomorrow, you'll be married."

Tomorrow? shouted Willow in her head. *Just like with the food pantry, we only have a few more hours! We still need to replace the missing desserts! Not to mention whip up a wedding present.*

"Married! Hitched! Tied the knot!" Willow said, hoping she sounded peppy instead of panicked. She and Delia shuffled over to the sink so that Cat and Mr. Henry would have to turn their bodies toward them and away from the dessert containers stacked nearby. If Cat looked too closely, she was bound to notice what was missing.

"Is there anything you two are really hoping for?" asked Delia. "You know, as a gift. Anything you really, *really* have your hearts set on? You can tell us. We're completely trustworthy."

Mr. Henry took off his hat—unlike the straw sun hat he wore all summer, this one was made of heavier material, like stiff felt—and ran his hand through his hair.

"You two ladies are family," he began. "There is no need to give us a gift to mark our exchange of vows." Then he put his hat right back onto his head again. "And of course we have the utmost faith in you both. Ms. Catherine and I know that you'll do all you can to help make our day tomorrow just perfect."

Willow couldn't stop the nervous hiccups that took over her throat.

"Perfect?"

Hiccup!

Willow could practically hear the ticking of the clock, counting down the minutes to their wedding. She didn't feel anywhere close to ready for it. In fact, she was beginning to feel like it might turn into another one of her disasters.

Suddenly, the faces of the kids at school appeared in her mind. The pointing, the laughing. The girl who spit her cupcake in a trash can. The boy who lost a tooth on his cookie. The teacher who told her to pack up all her plates and platters, and go home.

Willow hiccupped again, panic flaring up for real in her chest now. Should she and Delia just forget about trying to help with the wedding? Maybe they would be better off leaving everything to their big sisters. Violet and Darlene seemed to be able to handle the pressure. Maybe Delia and Willow should just skip the wedding entirely and go right back over to the food pantry instead?

Hiccup!

Delia shot her a look to quiet down.

Willow glanced at the window over the sink. If only the hummingbirds were around in winter. Instead, where was that Christmas magic Delia told her about?

Mr. Henry was still talking. "But as for a present, well, having Ms. Catherine agree to be my bride"— he tossed back the rest of his hot cocoa for courage, his cheeks flushed as red as Rudolph's nose—"well, that's all the gift I could ever want."

Ms. Catherine fanned herself with a leftover banana, and she told Mr. Henry he shouldn't say such sweet things. But Willow could tell that Cat was eating up every word of it.

Delia cleared her throat to get the happy couple back on track.

"Well, that's romantic and all. But could you be more specific?" she said, her eyebrows furrowing as she concentrated. "Is there something you really want? Something that someone could give you as a gift?"

"Like a delicious dish?" *Hiccup!* "Or maybe a favorite dessert?" suggested Willow. She stepped closer toward Cat and Mr. Henry, her nerves calming now. "Something chocolate or caramel or covered in rainbow sprinkles?"

"Or maybe a romantic dinner for two?" Delia asked, pressing in from the other side. "Perhaps you might like a fancy fish stew?"

And suddenly the two cousins were looming over Cat and Mr. Henry, pinching them in like garlic in a press. If they could just hit on the right thing, maybe Cat and Mr. Henry wouldn't care that the cousins had lost so many desserts!

But the happy couple barely seemed to notice.

They turned their gazes back onto each other with moony eyes.

"I can't think of a single thing we need, y'all," Cat sighed happily. "The way you girls have helped make all those cookies and treats, I already owe you so much. It's been a real pleasure to know you're both working so hard to make tomorrow a perfect day."

There it was again. That word: *perfect!* Willow pinched her lips tight to keep another panicky hiccup from bursting out.

"That can be your gift to Mr. Henry and me," Cat continued, giving their shoulders each a squeeze. "A perfect wedding day, y'all. We don't have kids of our own, so we're just inviting folks we know in town and you Bumpuses. It will be small in size. But with y'all's help, our wedding will be overflowing with good food!"

Dabbing a napkin at his cocoa mustache, Mr. Henry got up and set his mug in the sink. "Miss Delia and Miss Willow, there is a little something. If we could trouble you both for one more dessert," he said, and here he paused to look them both in the eye. He seemed to hesitate about asking them for a favor, even though tomorrow was one of the biggest days of his life. Willow gave him an eager smile—she was willing to do anything to make Cat and Mr. Henry happy.

"When you came in," Mr. Henry continued, unfolding a handwritten recipe on an old sheet of paper. "I was just telling Ms. Catherine about a favorite holiday treat. It was a Rickles family tradition, actually, something my brother, Roland, and I enjoyed every Christmas as children."

This was it. Finally, a gift idea that would thrill Cat and Mr. Henry! Willow and Delia leaned in a little closer to hear.

"Gingerbread."

Cat clapped her hands as if Mr. Henry had just revealed the secret to long-lasting bubble gum.

"So if I may, could I ask you to make a loaf to share at the wedding reception? Just a little nod to the Rickles family, for my brother and me?"

Delia said they'd be happy to make it, and Willow smiled in agreement. Gingerbread couldn't be that hard to make. It wasn't like a fancy, flaming dessert. Or a snapping, squirming dinner.

"I bet the wedding guests would love gingerbread," Willow said.

Then, a little more softly, she whispered, "That is, if it doesn't get snatched up by Santa's elves before it makes it to the wedding reception. . . ."

Delia gave her cousin a sharp nudge, which made Willow smack a hand over her mouth.

"She was just kidding," Delia announced, her hands waving nervously in the air like she was shooing a gnat. And grabbing Willow by the arm, she dragged her over to the far counter, where they could pull out the mixing bowls and measuring cups without being overheard.

Willow leaned in close to her cousin as they read through the ingredients to Mr. Henry's recipe.

"Now listen," Delia began, her voice determined,

"we're going to make these gingerbread loaves, and we'll keep a close eye on this kitchen tonight. Because if the Rickles family's favorite treat goes missing, Cat and Mr. Henry's special day will go from *perfect* to *pathetic*!"

Chapter 12
defending the desserts

It was a few hours later when Sweet William burst through the door into the Whispering Pines kitchen with big news. His curly hair was dusted with snow, which began to melt as he relayed his message.

"Dad says you better come over to Delia's house now because they've set the table and the Christmas Eve feasting is minutes away and we're opening presents once the meal is finished and I really want to see if I got that pet rat I asked for and whatever you need to do for the wedding can wait until tomorrow! So come on! Hurry up! Let's eat!"

And then he began to pant like Bernice after she'd chased a squirrel. Willow was pretty sure he hadn't stopped to take a single breath.

The cousins were pulling the gingerbread loaves from the oven. Willow promised they would come right over once they finished. Like Sweet William, she could hardly wait to get to the Christmas gifts, so she quickly turned off the heat and threw the dirty spoons into the sink.

"Cat, why don't you and Mr. Henry head over now too?" Delia suggested in her usual helpful way. "You deserve a break. Willow and I will clean up in here once we're done."

At the thought of finally getting to relax, Cat's face was clearly relieved. She untied her apron strings and turned to Mr. Henry, who was adding silver sprinkles to the wedding cake wherever Cat directed. In moments, they were out the door and into the snow with Sweet William.

Thwack!

"What did you do that for?" complained Willow,

picking up a sponge at the crowded sink. She stared at the tall stacks of dirty mixing bowls and measuring cups. "You heard Sweet William. We're having the Christmas Eve feast, like we do at Grandma and Grandpa's house in Chicago. And when we're done eating, we open presents!"

Delia's head was inside a cabinet now, and her voice came out muffled. Willow could tell she was saying something about being helpful. But sometimes Willow didn't feel like being helpful. Sometimes Willow felt like leaving behind a mess for someone else to clean up!

As Willow glooped soap onto the sponge and started scrubbing, Delia pulled containers and lids from the cabinet.

"We need to be sure this gingerbread makes it to tomorrow's wedding," Delia explained. "Once it cools, we'll slice it up and seal it tight. Then we'll put it with what's left of the other desserts."

The cousins stared over at the stack of desserts they would serve at tomorrow's wedding. Willow counted the containers. Would it be enough to feed all the guests? Would Cat be disappointed?

She felt her stomach somersault. Was this another disaster in the making? Willow imagined all the wedding guests—including Cat and Mr. Henry and the whole family—standing there with empty plates and rumbling stomachs. Would they blame Willow and Delia?

"I'm glad Mr. Henry and Cat went ahead with Sweet William," Delia said, her voice calm and clear like a crossing guard's. Though if Willow remembered right, Delia wasn't a crossing guard at her school anymore. She was a library monitor. "I didn't want them to overhear our plan."

Willow's ears perked up. She didn't know they had a plan! Would they stay up all night, whipping up more wedding desserts to replace the missing ones? Would they look for tiny footprints in the snow to track down Santa's elves and the stolen treats?

"When the celebrating is over," Delia continued, "we should come back in here with sleeping bags and spend the night. We have to defend our desserts!"

Willow's eyes fell on Cat's beautiful wedding cake at the back counter, the silver sprinkles catching in the light. What if something happened to Cat's cake? They needed to protect more than just the wedding treats tonight!

Willow's stomach stopped somersaulting. Now it felt like it had climbed up in her throat! She could hardly get the words out.

"You're right, Delia. . . . We slept under the table in the summertime, so we can do it again tonight. Nothing and nobody will mess with our kitchen!"

Once the stack of dirty dishes was finally clean (or clean *enough*, Willow decided), the two cousins dashed across the wintery yard toward Delia's yellow house and the Christmas Eve feast. Flakes the size of quarters swirled in the crisp air like they were caught in a snow globe, drifting onto the cousins' hats and in their hair and helping decorate Sweet William's special pine tree. And the bright colors of the twinkly Christmas lights in both yards gave off a warm glow.

The knots in Willow's stomach eased just a bit, and she felt like she was at the North Pole.

"Who knows, Delia, maybe while we're defending desserts tonight, we'll have time to make something extra fancy to give Cat and Mr. Henry as our wedding gift. We could stay up cooking the whole night!"

But when she looked over at her cousin, Delia was gazing out at the water and the thick gray clouds hanging low over the horizon. "A blizzard's coming," she said. "It's going to be a white Christmas!"

Bubbly-as-Willow & Sweet-as-Delia Holiday Punch

Ingredients:

1 12-ounce container frozen lemonade concentrate, defrosted until mushy

4 cups red fruit juice (Willow likes raspberry or cherry; Delia likes cranberry or strawberry)

Ice

3 cups fizzy ginger ale

Sprigs of fresh mint

Directions:

1. Make sure you have an adult's help.

2. Using a large pitcher or punch bowl, pour in the lemonade concentrate, and add the proper amount of water (about 3 cans). Mix together.

3. Add the red fruit juice and ice.

4. Just before serving, pour in the ginger ale to make it nice and fizzy. Then add sprigs of green mint to the punch bowl or in each glass.

5. Make a toast to your cousins, and enjoy!

Makes about 12 servings.

Chapter 13
a full table of holiday cheer

"M erry Christmas, everyone! Let the feasting begin," announced Uncle Delvan from one end of the long table, which was actually three or four tables pushed together. Grandma was seated at the other end, and together they were directing traffic as plates and side dishes and mounds of turkey and ham and vegetable casserole made their way from hand to hand.

"I think we need to raise a glass of cheer for today's chefs: Grandpa along with Delvan, Liam, and Jonathan," said Grandma, her goblet of bubbly red-and-green punch raised in the air. "They've done a great job making sure everyone—vegetarians and carnivores—has something special to eat tonight."

And Willow and the rest of the cousins and aunts and uncles and grandparents began clinking glasses with each other, including honorary Bumpus family members Cat, Mr. Henry, and Reverend Rickles.

"And don't forget the other chefs," reminded Cat, getting to her feet for her own toast. "I want to make sure we give a cheer for Delia and Willow, who have

been my helpers in the kitchen next door, y'all. I can relax now, knowing that tomorrow's wedding is in their capable hands."

Willow's fork suddenly slipped through her fingers and onto her plate with a noisy *clang*. At the same time, Delia accidentally knocked over her glass of punch. It hit the table at an angle, then sloshed onto the bright red tablecloth before she caught it. Gasps rang out around the table like a choir of startled angels.

"Maybe our hands," Willow whispered in her cousin's direction, "aren't nearly as capable as Cat thinks!"

The rest of the meal was spent in happy Christmas cheer, with platters passed from one family member to the next. Though Sweet William's announcement that he was a vegetarian too, just like Delia, was met with some doubt.

"If you're a vegetarian, you have to eat vegetables, Sweet William," pointed out Violet. "You can't just eat bread and cheese."

"Maybe I'm a bread-and-cheese-tarian instead,"

he decided, pushing away the plate of green beans Willow was offering. "Or a dinner-roll-tarian."

Willow couldn't help but cast a suspicious eye on her sister and Darlene. Somebody made off with the wedding desserts—could it have been them? Violet was competitive, but would she and Darlene really stoop so low? Willow chomped down on her green beans and stared across the table. Maybe she and Delia should check their sisters' bedroom.

"What have you two been up to all day?" Delia asked Darlene and Violet, clearly sharing Willow's suspicions. "Been hungry for some cookies? That's not powdered sugar I see on your shirt there, Darlene, is it?"

Violet and Darlene rolled their eyes to the ceiling and explained that they'd been rehearsing for the wedding all day. "We're performing the wedding march, as you already know. And we were practicing the amazing song we wrote for Cat and Mr. Henry," Violet whispered, making sure no one else overheard. "They're going to love our gift the most."

"And the white stuff on my shirt?" added Darlene. "It's baby powder. Violet and I helped dress the triplets for dinner tonight. Because you two were off goofing somewhere and no help to anyone."

Willow thought that if Santa Claus were around to overhear their big sisters' tone, he certainly would strike them off the "Nice" list and move them over to "Naughty."

"Why do you even ask?" wondered Violet, leaning forward in her chair and staring hard at Willow and Delia. "Did something happen in the kitchen again? Are you two hiding something?"

Delia and Willow waved them off. They acted busy with a platter of veggie casserole, turning their suspicions elsewhere around the table. Everyone seemed to be enjoying the feasting, especially the triplets, who gummed their dinners with obvious enthusiasm from their three high chairs. And Willow was relieved to see that someone had taken away Baby June's spoon.

The triplets were even more enthusiastic for what

came after dinner, when the whole family gathered beside the big Christmas tree to exchange presents. It was another Bumpus tradition Willow was excited to teach them! She couldn't decide what June, July, and August liked more: the sparkly ornaments on the tree, the wrapping paper and boxes, or the actual gifts themselves.

Once all the presents were opened—Willow's favorite was a new apron from Cat, Delia's was a book on bird-watching from Willow's mom—Grandpa and the uncles brought out a few homemade pies and a tub of ice cream.

"I saved up these blueberries from the summertime, when the grandkids and I picked them during our vacation and then I froze them," Grandpa began. "Delvan, Liam, and Jonathan here thawed them out and baked them into pies this afternoon so that we could have a little taste of summer right now in December. I hope you enjoy!"

Once the slices were placed onto each dessert plate beside a dollop of vanilla ice cream, Mr. Henry got to his feet. He looked nervous as he removed his winter hat and placed it back onto his head a few times. Willow heard him clear his throat once or twice.

"Before the evening is over," Mr. Henry began shyly, "I just want to take a few moments to say thank you. The blueberries of summer are a perfect example of all that is wonderful about Whispering Pines and now Delvan and Deenie's lovely yellow house. When the whole Bumpus family is here, picking blueberries or camping out in the yard, it is a time of great joy.

"And joy is what I am so grateful for. Your family has made me one of its members, and Ms. Catherine and my brother now too. And you've allowed us to share in your joy. You've never been ones to focus on material things, which pass away with time. You celebrate each other. And with Christmas here, that feels like the true meaning of this season: joy in being together."

Sniffles erupted around the room as Grandma and Aunt Rosie wiped their eyes, and Aunt Deenie and Willow's mom blew their noses. Even Uncle

Jonathan was dabbing his tears with one of the triplets' blankets, trying to collect himself.

Willow decided now was her time to ask again. Maybe with all the Christmas magic in the air, her parents would finally give in.

"If we lived here all year long like Delia, we could have these kinds of celebrations all the time," she began. "What do you think, Mom and Dad? Can we just forget about Chicago and stay here forever?"

But before Willow could hear an answer, Cat got to her feet. She was dabbing a tissue to her eyes with one hand and fanning herself with a candy cane in the other.

"I don't want to start fussing like a mother hen over her baby chicks," she said, a sniffle breaking up her announcement. "But Henry Rickles, you're so sweet, I want to stir you into my coffee! Y'all, Henry is right. This Bumpus family makes us feel so loved. Now I'm going to say good night and head upstairs to bed for some beauty sleep. I'll see everyone tomorrow at the weddin'! Merry Christmas, y'all!"

And with hugs and pats on the back and wishes of holiday cheer, Mr. Henry and half the family headed out into the falling snow to spend the night at Whispering Pines. The other half turned out the lights and followed Cat up the staircase for the bedrooms in the cozy yellow house.

"Sweet William, what about leaving out a plate of cookies for Santa and his reindeer?" asked Willow. "Don't you want to convince Santa to stay here for a while and take a rest?"

Sweet William yawned as he slowly headed for the back door. "Sure, you can leave Santa some blueberry pie," he called back over his shoulder. "But don't worry about the reindeer, I've already got them covered!"

Chapter 14
starlight and snowflakes

Willow and Delia waited up in Delia's room until the house was nice and quiet. They stretched out on the floor and peered out the window at the starry night sky, watching for flying reindeer and a bright red sleigh to pass overhead. Then, tiptoeing down the creaky staircase and past the Christmas tree with its sparkly ornaments, they slipped silently into their coats and boots. In a flash, they were out the back door and crossing through the yard, the new-fallen snow like fluffy pillows beneath their feet.

"This is beautiful," whispered Delia as they took their time following the path that connected the

Arts & Eats Café to Whispering Pines. "Look at the lights on Mr. Henry's hobby shed. With the snow everywhere, doesn't it look like a postcard?"

"It looks like a painting your dad might make," Willow agreed. "Let's go around front and peek at your house too."

They trudged up the path toward the front of the café. Off to one side were the pine trees that gave Whispering Pines its name. Sweet William's popcorn garlands zigzagged through the branches of the biggest tree. And the Christmas balls made of pinecones and birdseed swung from snowy boughs here and there.

"My little brother really went all out for this tree, didn't he?" Willow said.

"And did you notice his reindeer feeders?" asked Delia. "They're everywhere."

Willow looked around, really focusing this time, and that's when she caught sight of the long orange carrots hanging from branches like colorful icicles. Green celery, too. They were dangling from trees all

around the two yards like healthy holiday ornaments.

"The decorations your parents put up are pretty amazing too," Willow said, stepping toward the front of Delia's yard and the old-fashioned red sleigh parked there. "The garland and the lights—all of it looks so beautiful."

Delia agreed. "I've been so busy thinking about the food pantry the past few weeks, I didn't even pay attention to all the Christmas decorations my mom and dad hung around here. But when you come back into town, Willow, it's like I start to see things through your eyes. And suddenly everything looks special!"

Willow climbed up into the bright red sleigh and scooted over to make room for Delia beside her. Then they snuggled in close for warmth.

"Over summer vacation, I've imagined what it would be like living here at Whispering Pines," said Willow, looking up into the sky for a star to wish on. "But being here at Christmas, well, I feel it now more than ever. And not just because of the bad stuff that happened at school. If I lived here with you, Delia, then every day would be special.

"I keep thinking of that Christmas song we always hear playing on the radio. About walking in a winter wonderland. Just look around us—this place really *is* a winter wonderland!"

Delia said she hoped Willow could convince her parents to leave Chicago. "Even though I still think you have to face what happened at school, I don't want you to give up," she said, nudging Willow's shoulder playfully. "Tell Uncle Liam and Aunt Aggie it's the only gift you want this year from Santa Claus!"

"Do you think Santa would take Violet and Darlene if I begged him?"

Delia laughed, her breath like crystals in the freezing air. "He could put them both to work writing songs at the North Pole!"

Willow looked back up at the shimmering jewel box of stars above them. She burrowed in closer to her cousin, and they both were silent, drinking in the beauty of the wintery yard. Willow held her breath

and listened to the heavy quiet. She could actually hear the snowflakes landing on her coat. Delia was catching them in her mittened hands and examining their shapes in the faint light.

"They really are different," Delia whispered, as if she were looking through a microscope. "Each little snowflake is different from the next. I'd heard that, but had never seen it for myself."

Willow smiled, her cheeks nearly frozen from the

cold. No matter what she and her cousin were doing, Delia always found a way to make it brainy.

"I don't know a lot about snowflakes," Willow said, suddenly feeling that somersaulting panic in her stomach again. "But I do know Cat's wedding is tomorrow! Come on, Delia, let's get cooking!"

Climbing off the red sleigh and looping their arms together, the cousins leaned into the freezing wind off the lake and pushed on toward the Whispering Pines kitchen.

"Somehow I will convince my family to move," Willow vowed. "I want to be here every single day of the year, not just a few times now and then. It's not enough!"

Delia didn't have to say a word. She gave Willow's arm a quick squeeze. And Willow knew exactly what she meant.

Chapter 15
on the lookout for elves

This is a good sign!" Delia said as she tugged off her snow boots and tucked them into the corner. "The gingerbread loaves are still here. All of them!"

Willow and Delia got busy cutting the loaves into even slices. Then they sealed them up in containers so they would be fresh and ready for tomorrow's wedding.

"Think about it, Delia. Everyone keeps saying Santa's elves are to blame for the disappearing desserts," Willow whispered, her eyes darting suspiciously around the kitchen. "And tonight is Christmas Eve, the busiest night of the year—if you're an elf!"

The cousins crossed their hearts and promised they'd keep a watchful eye on the treats tonight so nothing else would go missing.

Tiptoeing upstairs, they gathered pillows and blankets and their warmest pajamas, somehow avoiding detection by mothers, fathers, and curious siblings who had already climbed into bed for the night. The only sounds came from the living room, where Mr. Henry and Reverend Rickles were having a quiet conversation by the fireplace. Willow could smell the aroma of fresh-brewed coffee.

When she and Delia reached Sweet William's door on the second floor, they peered inside. "Sweet William," whispered Willow, though Delia kept shushing her to speak more softly, "do you think we could borrow Bernice tonight? We need her help keeping watch over the kitchen."

Sweet William poked his head out from under a blanket he'd rigged up like a fort near the window. His flashlight thumped onto the floor, throwing shadows on the wall as Bernice and Gossie poked their heads out beside him. Willow could hear the low humming of Bill, Pat, and Jimmy on the other side of the blanket.

"Nope, can't give her up, Willow," he said. "She's helping me and Gossie read bedtime stories to the baby geese. Plus, I need Bernice to keep a lookout for Santa's sleigh. It's part of an important experiment I'm doing."

Delia and Willow dragged their blankets and pillows down the stairs. They crept back toward the kitchen without drawing the attention of Mr. Henry or Reverend Rickles in the living room. And somehow, they managed not to hit any of the creaky floorboards.

"Sweet William is trying to catch Santa's reindeer," Willow said, tossing their sleeping supplies under the kitchen table. "And we're trying to catch Santa's elves. Who do you think is crazier? Sweet William or us?"

"Everybody in our family seems a little crazy," admitted Delia. "But that's what makes being a Bumpus so great."

Willow turned her focus to the containers of desserts stacked up along the back countertop. There were half the number of sugar cookies, half the snowballs, half the peppermint bark, half the chocolate-dipped pretzels, half the cheesecake squares. Only the Rickles family favorite, the gingerbread loaves, were in full supply.

"We should put the gingerbread between us tonight," Willow said. "There's no way both of us can sleep through an elf invasion, is there?"

Delia slid the two boxes under the kitchen table, right beside their blankets and pillows. Then she went back and gathered up all the rest of the wedding desserts as well. She and Willow stacked the boxes on either side of their bedding, making what looked like a food fortress.

"What about Cat's cake?" asked Willow. "We have to keep it safe!"

"We shouldn't touch it," warned Delia. "What if we break it?"

Willow thought for a minute, then bounced a few times in her socks.

"What if we put a fence around it? Like an alarm that would alert us to elves!"

So both cousins pulled out glasses and mugs from the tall cabinets and lined them up, side by side, around the cake. Then they added forks and spoons into each one, creating a rattling fortress to guard Cat's masterpiece.

"That should do it," Willow said hopefully. "If elves try to get to that cake, we'll hear it!"

Now the cousins were ready to do some cooking. But their list of what they needed to make had grown longer and longer over the past few days. Delia's eyebrows knit in concentration, and Willow's confidence began to sag.

"Okay, if we're going to make Cat's wedding really amazing, this is the time to do it," Delia said, putting her hands on Willow's shoulders and squaring off for a pep talk. "We've already saved one wedding with our cooking, Willow. And we've saved a café, too. Not to mention impressed a food critic and landed on the front page of a newspaper. We're amazing chefs!"

Willow nodded, but she wasn't completely convinced. "We can do anything," she said, though her words lacked a certain bounce. "Right?"

Delia gave Willow's shoulders a squeeze. "Come on, Willow! Of course right!"

Willow felt a spark of excitement catch in her stomach. "We just have to set our minds to it."

"And believe in ourselves," added Delia.

"And be creative," Willow chirped.

"And measure things!" reminded Delia.

"And not do anything stupid!" they said at the same time.

So for the next long while, as the snow piled up in drifts all around the house and the yellow light from the kitchen shone out into the dark yard, the cousins kept as busy as . . . well, elves on Christmas Eve. Santa himself would have been impressed.

"We finished making more of the peppermint bark, the chocolate-dipped pretzels, and the sugar cookies. I think we can call it a night now," said Delia a while later as she stirred another pot of hot cocoa. Her words stretched out sleepily, interrupted by a few yawns. "We're in better shape for the wedding, don't you think?"

Willow was at the counter, lining up fresh bowls and whisks and ingredients.

"There's one thing I keep thinking about, Delia. And that's our gift."

Delia said they'd already made the gingerbread, and it was safely resting between their blankets and pillows for the night. "It's what Mr. Henry asked for, you know." And she yawned again.

"Plus," Delia added sleepily, "I don't have the ingredients to make the fancy fish soup. And you don't have what you need for the fancy dessert. Do you?"

Willow smiled and offered Delia a whisk.

"I do! *We* do, Delia!" she said, a new wave of energy putting a little spring in her stirring. "Everybody thinks chocolate soufflés are hard to make. But look at this recipe! There are only a few simple ingredients. And they're right here!"

Delia poured the hot cocoa and joined Willow at the counter.

"I know how much this means to you, Willow. So I'll do it. Just elbow me now and then if I fall asleep."

Delia took a seat on one of the stools and began mixing. Before long, her blinks became slower and slower. But Willow, on the other hand, was as focused as a scientist—she'd never been more exact in her mixing and measuring as she was now. She needed their dessert to taste delicious—not only for Cat's sake, but for her own.

"This is it," Willow said a short while later. She turned on the oven light and stared through the tiny window at the round white baking dish. Her eyes were growing heavy with exhaustion now too.

"This soufflé will be better than our sisters' song, better than Grandma's fancy carriage, even better than your parents' painting, Delia. This dessert will be Cat's favorite gift of all, I just know it."

Delia yawned as she flicked off the overhead light, leaving the kitchen in the yellow glow of the oven.

She mumbled sleepily about the long, busy day. Then she wrapped up inside her blanket like a caterpillar in its chrysalis, patted the gingerbread's boxy containers on the floor beside her, and dropped her head onto her pillow.

When the oven beeped a short while later, letting them know the soufflé was done, Delia didn't even stir. Willow climbed to her feet and shuffled over to the oven, the yellow glow like a candle shining into the dark, fragrant kitchen. Pulling the soufflé out with her thick oven mitts, Willow felt a dreamy excitement begin to rise in her chest. The soufflé looked impressive—a towering chocolate cloud!

"Delia, look at this!" she whispered. "It's nearly as big as Bernice's head!" But she knew her cousin was already asleep.

With the warm soufflé safely settled on the countertop, Willow climbed under her blanket beside Delia at the table to sleep for the night. Willow snuggled in, feeling her whole body relax at last as she closed her eyes. "Finally, Delia, we did it."

There weren't too many hours left of this night before Christmas. And all through the house, no creatures were stirring that Willow knew about. Not even a mouse.

Pffssst.

Or was that one? Willow's eyes shot open. She listened closely. It was a faint hissing sound, low and slow. Then silence.

Pffssst. There it was again.

At first, she told herself it was the *whoosh* of the wind outside, swirling the snow. But then she began to think that the slow *pffssst* was coming from inside the kitchen. Was that the sound a mouse made when it found a good dessert? Or was it a hungry gosling? Maybe Bill, Pat, or Jimmy nibbling on a snack?

She quickly sat up, whacking her head into the kitchen table.

The *pffssst* was clearer now. Willow got to her feet, following the sound around the room. It wasn't at the refrigerator, wasn't at the door, wasn't at the back counter. It was coming from the countertop, right where she'd set her chocolate soufflé to cool.

Pffssst.

Rather than turn on the overhead lights, Willow flipped the switch at the oven and let the soft yellow light shine into the kitchen again.

She stared at her soufflé. It was more than just cooling now. It was collapsing in on itself! And with one final *pffssst*, Willow and Delia's wedding gift seemed to heave its last breath. What was left looked like a flat tire.

Willow turned off the oven light and dove back under her covers, hiding her whole head under her pillow. She squeezed her eyes shut, pushing out the thoughts of yet another baking disaster. The only good part of the situation was that there was nobody awake to laugh at her.

Maybe, just maybe, she and Delia would get up in the morning and discover their own Christmas miracle.

Chapter 16
sweet william's surprise

The sky was dark blue when Delia and Willow stirred the next morning. Sweet William was standing in the kitchen near the table, talking breathlessly and frantically trying to pull on his snow boots.

"And there's a big one near the bluff staircase who's probably Dasher. I think the one closest to the porch here is Dancer, or maybe it's Prancer. I always mix those two up. . . ."

Willow sat up, careful not to whack her head into the table. Bernice greeted her with a slobbery lick on the nose, tail wagging excitedly. Gossie let out an eager honk, and Bill, Pat, and Jimmy flapped their wings.

Even though the sun hadn't even peeped into the sky, Christmas morning seemed to be in full swing. Willow put her hand on Delia's shoulder and shook her awake.

"I was dreaming I had a goose-feather blanket," Delia said, letting out a few quick sneezes. "Wouldn't that be so warm and cozy?" And she tried to pull her covers back over her shoulder.

"Delia, it's Christmas morning! This is no time for sleeping in," Willow said with a hint of exasperation. "Aren't you usually the early riser? And I'm the one who won't wake up? Come on, let's get a move on, Sleeping Beauty!"

Willow scrambled to her feet, then stuck her hand out to help Delia up. Once they were standing and able to shake off the stiffness from their night on the kitchen floor, Willow turned to Sweet William.

"What are you talking about *Dancer* and *Prancer*?"

"I knew it'd work, Willow! I knew I could get

them to stay," Sweet William was saying as he zipped up his winter coat. "Let's get outside, quick! We've got to find Santa before he moves on!"

Willow looked at Delia, who raised a single eyebrow back. Neither seemed to have any idea what Sweet William was talking about.

"Slow down a minute," Willow said, putting her hand on her little brother's wool hat. His crazy curls were sticking out from under it, coiling in every direction.

"What do you mean *get them to stay*?" asked Delia, who was giving Bernice's ears a sleepy scratching. "Willow and I don't know who you mean by *them*."

"I mean THEM!" Sweet William said, pointing out the window and into the snowy yard. "Santa's reindeer! Let's go!"

And he stepped toward the door to let himself out. But at the same moment, Willow and Delia dove for the doorknob, blocking Sweet William's way.

"You can't go out there," gasped Willow, staring into the yard. There were animals out there. Big ones.

With antlers! "Just look at them! They're huge!"

"They're real!" added Delia, her eyes wide in disbelief.

"They're reindeer!" they said in unison.

There were so many things to take in, Willow couldn't decide where to look first. The reindeer were munching on the carrots and celery Sweet William had hung from the trees throughout the yard. There must have been seven, maybe eight animals scattered across the grounds, near the houses, and on the far side where the blueberries grew in summer.

"H-h-how?" was all Delia could manage, her finger pointing from one reindeer to the next.

Willow had no idea what time it was as she peered through the windows. The reindeer's dark brown coats stood out against the endless snow, which seemed pale blue in the early morning light. Snowdrifts were piled so high, they climbed to the porch. She looked around for Grandma's iron bench, the one she had given to Grandpa in the summer, but the snow seemed to have swallowed it up.

"You were right, Delia. We had a blizzard, just like you said." Willow nodded, her hands on Sweet William's shoulders. She held tight to her little brother, both from the shock of seeing reindeer feeding in the yard but also to keep him from racing out there and scaring them off.

Or, knowing Sweet William, climbing onto their backs for a ride.

Delia mumbled something about liking to study clouds and weather maps, but her voice trailed off. She was too stunned by the enormous animals in the yard to talk about blizzards and predicting storms.

"H-h-how?" she stuttered again.

"I just put out the treats," Sweet William explained, taking Delia's hand in his small, gloved one. "But now that they're here, you've got to let me get out there and look for Santa. I need to catch him before he takes off to deliver more Christmas presents. And before we have to get ready for the wedding."

That seemed to snap Delia back to her senses.

"The wedding!" she gasped, turning to Willow.

"We've got to hurry and get dressed, then come back over here to help. Cat's going to need us to set up all the food. What are we waiting for?"

And Delia began throwing on the layers of her winter clothing, jamming her feet into her big boots and her head into her wool hat.

"Let's leave Bernice and the geese inside," Willow said, snapping into action too. "We don't want them scaring off the reindeer."

"But we can't leave them here, in the kitchen," warned Delia, "all alone with the wedding desserts and Cat's cake. We've already had one wedding disaster with Bernice eating the food!"

Delia's eyes darted around the floor beneath the table, like she was looking for something. And Willow knew just what it was: the gingerbread boxes! Willow picked up the blankets and pillows, but she couldn't find them either.

"The gingerbread. It's not on the floor, not on the counter," Willow said, her voice rising to a shout. "Not on the table! Not under the table!"

"I don't believe it," Delia said, shaking her head. "Santa's elves slipped past us again last night! Those sneaky little trolls don't need kids to set out cookies by the fireplace on Christmas Eve! Not when they steal treats from places like our kitchen!"

"The cake!" shrieked Willow.

She and Delia raced to the back counter. And to their huge relief, the wedding cake sat safely behind its dishware fence.

"Cat's wedding cake is fine," Delia said. "But look at that!"

She was pointing at the collapsed soufflé, which appeared more like a melted hockey puck than anything edible. "The elves even let the air out of your cake!"

Willow stopped in her tracks. And while she was breathless thinking about the missing gingerbread and protecting Cat's wedding cake and sneaky elves, suddenly she began to giggle. And the giggling grew into laughter. And the laughter into a snorting, shoulder-shaking roar.

"You're right, Delia," she managed to say. "It looks like a flat tire!"

And now the two of them were laughing, and even Sweet William joined in. Only this laughter wasn't the hurtful kind that Willow endured at the school bake sale. This time, it felt okay to laugh at herself.

"I don't know what happened to the desserts. But let's get over to the Arts and Eats Café," Willow announced. "I want to take a look at the Christmas tree and see if Santa left any presents. If he really stopped here last night, then maybe we'll start to understand what's going on with his reindeer."

"Right," agreed Sweet William, pushing his way onto the porch. "Santa has a lot of explaining to do!"

Chapter 17
anything is possible at christmas

They slipped into the yard, quiet as snowflakes. Willow and Delia each took hold of one of Sweet William's hands, carefully stepping as far from the reindeer as possible to avoid startling them. Most of the males looked taller than Delia, and Willow thought their antlers would be dangerous to touch. The females were easy to spot, their beautiful ears twitching, heads free of the heavy horns.

"I can hardly walk in this snow," whispered Delia, her laughter quiet so she wouldn't scare off the herd. "It's up to my thighs!"

By the time they reached the front door of Delia's

yellow house, their legs were freezing from the deep drifts and their teeth were chattering. They let themselves in, trying hard not to wake the quiet house.

Once their boots and coats were off, they sprinted over to the Christmas tree. Even though Willow knew they should be patient for the whole family to wake up before checking their presents, neither she nor Delia nor Sweet William could wait.

"This year is different," Delia reasoned logically. "With Cat and Mr. Henry's wedding at noon, we have to hurry everything up. And that means a quick peek at the gifts!"

"I think you're right," agreed Willow with the same businesslike tone. "And we need to get to the bottom of a couple things. Like why Santa's reindeer are munching veggies in the yard, and whether his elves stole our desserts!"

Sweet William didn't need any prompting, so they dove into the mound of gifts, looking for ones with their names. Willow found hers right away: Santa brought her a waffle iron. "Exactly what I asked for!"

Delia got a telescope for gazing at the stars. And Santa gave Sweet William a spy kit, which Willow thought couldn't be a more appropriate present.

"We need to get dressed for the wedding now," Delia said as they turned for the staircase. "But we can't let you go outside, Sweet William. Those animals are too big. You could get hurt."

Willow had an idea. "Maybe you could use Delia's

binoculars, if that's okay," she suggested, her eyes on Delia. Her cousin nodded and pointed toward the counter near the cash register, where the binoculars were sitting.

"Take them upstairs along with your new spy kit," Delia directed. "If you sit at my window, you can look down into the yard and study the reindeer from up there. Who knows, you might be able to spot Santa Claus too."

Sweet William seemed to like the idea, and he looped the binoculars around his neck and took off up the staircase in pursuit of Santa. The girls tiptoed after him, whispering the whole way.

"Those cannot be reindeer," Delia was saying. "I think they're elk. We studied them in my zoology club, and from what I remember, elk look a lot like reindeer. Plus, Michigan has tons of them. But no reindeer."

"I don't know, Delia," Willow was saying as they carried their junior bridesmaid dresses into the bathroom to get dressed. "There's a chance they could be Santa's, right? I mean, look at the facts: There are presents under the Christmas tree. The gingerbread went missing last night, and Santa's elves are known for being really sneaky. And we have a yard full of reindeer!"

"Elk!" corrected Delia.

Though as Delia peered out the bathroom window at the beautiful animals nibbling the carrots and celery, her expression softened.

She turned back to Willow, one eyebrow raised practically to the ceiling.

"The logical explanation is elk. But Willow, you don't really think . . ."

"You're the one who's been saying it, Delia," she answered, stepping to the window beside her cousin. "Christmas magic! It makes anything possible. Even reindeer!"

They were back down the stairs in moments, teeth brushed, faces washed ("Does wiped quickly with a wet towel count?" wondered Willow), and dresses on.

Willow loved the soft feel of the velvet fabric. Rather than the hideous pink flower-girl dresses from Aunt Rosie's wedding, these gowns were a deep Christmas green. "They match the pine trees," said Delia with an approving nod. "It's like we're woodland fairies!"

Both girls had tied matching green ribbons in their hair, though Willow's curls looked a little too wild, Delia told her. "Just let me calm them down with some water." And after a few minutes of touching up here and there, both cousins were in good enough shape to walk down the aisle at Cat's wedding.

"I'm sorry we won't have a wedding present to give Cat and Mr. Henry," Willow began. "It wasn't the elves who flattened our soufflé. It just sort of—"

And she tried to re-create the sound a soufflé makes when it's deflating. But her *pffssst* was interrupted by the *rrrrring!* of the café phone. Both cousins jumped in surprise.

Delia dashed for the cash register, where the phone hung from the wall. She answered it before the second ring.

"It's Reverend Rickles," she whispered to Willow. "He sounds worried."

Delia stared into Willow's face as she listened on the line, nodding now and then.

"What's the matter?" Willow whispered back.

"Oh, no," Delia gasped. "Go on. . . ."

Willow couldn't stand the suspense. She stepped closer and pressed her head against Delia's and the phone. Willow could just make out what Reverend Rickles was saying. Something about the blizzard . . . collapsing the food pantry roof . . . knocking out power . . . nowhere to feed the hungry today.

"He needs us," Delia whispered, her hand covering the mouthpiece. But Willow didn't have to be reminded. She already knew what was at stake.

That it was Christmas morning.

That more than a hundred people needed to be fed.

That today was the biggest event of the food pantry's whole year.

"But Cat needs us too," she reminded Delia.

And the two cousins stared hard into each other's faces. Willow scanned Delia's expression—saw her forehead furrowed with worry lines, her lips pinched tight in concentration.

Delia studied Willow right back.

"We can't choose between them," whispered Delia.

Willow waited just a single beat. "Then let's do both!"

Their gazes locked now, Willow and Delia looked closely into each other's amber eyes. Same color, same shape, same way of seeing things. And sometimes, in moments just like this one, the amber eyes worked a bit of their own magic, making Willow and Delia feel closer than cousins, stronger than sisters, even bigger than best friends.

"Send everybody here," Delia said, turning back to the phone and Reverend Rickles. Her voice sounded clear and calm. "The wedding isn't until noon. That gives us plenty of time to serve the Christmas breakfast. We can do it!"

Willow could hear Reverend Rickles asking what Cat thought about it. Was she okay with the idea? And Mr. Henry too? This was their special day, after all.

"Wh-what does Cat think?" stammered Delia, her eyes blinking. A long, heavy pause hung in the air. "*Um*, she . . . Well, she . . ."

"I'm happier than a bull-frog at a leapin' contest," Willow blurted into the phone, doing her best Cat impersonation. "You know, playin' leapfrog . . ."

Delia smacked her forehead and tugged the phone away. Had Willow just blown it? Did Reverend Rickles know that was Willow and not his future sister-in-law?

"Well, I am so relieved," the cousins heard him say with a deep sigh. "Cat, I always knew you were a generous soul, but good gravy! This is just tremendous. I see why my brother fell in love with you. You're a big-hearted lady."

Delia said a quick good-bye to Reverend Rickles and hung up the phone.

Then the cousins began biting their fingers, tugging their hair, pacing back and forth, and taking deep breaths over what they'd just agreed to. But there was no turning back.

"Violet has been telling me I have to face things," began Willow, fidgeting with the sash of her junior bridesmaid gown. "I think this is what she means, Delia. Today is the day we show everybody what we can do. We'll make this a special Christmas for the food pantry *and* for Cat and Mr. Henry."

Delia pulled on her braids, looking nervously out the window toward Whispering Pines, where the wedding was to take place in a few hours.

"I'm not sure where to start," she began. "Let's think this through. We need to have some sort of food along with drinks ready. In about two hours. For more than a hundred people!"

They stared around the Arts & Eats Café's shiny silver kitchen, their eyes wandering from the stove to the oven to the refrigerator. Willow searched frantically for inspiration. Delia blinked a few times, like she was just as stunned.

Finally, Willow's gaze landed on Cat's waffle iron, and she let out a whoop.

"Waffles!" she shouted. "We can use the café's waffle iron and the one Santa brought me! Waffles are all right, aren't they?"

"Are you kidding? Everybody knows waffles are just as good as pancakes! And the way we'll make them," Delia said, finally sounding confident again, "maybe even better!"

Delia & Willow's Christmas Miracle Waffles

Ingredients:

2 cups milk
2 tablespoons vinegar
2 cups flour
2 tablespoons sugar
2 teaspoons baking soda

½ teaspoon salt
2 egg yolks
4 tablespoons butter, melted
2 egg whites
1 teaspoon vanilla

Directions:

1. Make sure you have an adult's help.

2. In a medium-sized bowl, make the sour milk. Pour in just less than 2 cups of milk, then add 2 tablespoons vinegar.

3. Set this bowl aside for a few minutes.

4. In a separate bowl, mix together the flour, sugar, baking soda, and salt.

5. Once the milk has turned, stir in the egg yolks, melted butter, and vanilla into the bowl.

6. Combine the wet ingredients in with the dry.

7. Heat the waffle iron, then grease with butter or cooking oil.

8. Using a clean whisk, whip up the egg whites in their own clean bowl until frothy. Then add them to the batter until they are mixed in.

9. Spoon the batter onto the waffle iron and close the lid. Cook until golden brown, about 4 minutes.

10. Dribble with maple syrup, and enjoy!

Makes 4 to 6 servings.

Chapter 18
waffles and worry

Tugging their aprons over their heads, the cousins pulled Willow's brand-new waffle iron out of its box and lined it up on the countertop next to the Arts & Eats Café's well-worn waffle maker. Willow let out a sigh of relief that the café was closed today. Otherwise Cat's iron would be busy making waffles for customers.

Delia began pouring ingredients into a big bowl. A cloud of white flour puffed into the air as she barked out orders. Willow picked up a whisk and another bowl and joined her.

"Vanilla is next!" Willow hollered, cracking

eggs and tossing the shells into the trash can. Delia grabbed the bottle of vanilla and measured precisely for them both.

"Now stir!" she called.

Both cousins began churning their batter as quickly as they could.

"What's this?" came Uncle Delvan's voice from the hallway. "Looks like you two are whipping up a holiday surprise. Merry Christmas, girls!"

And he gave them each a quick peck on the cheek as he shuffled sleepily toward the coffeemaker to start a fresh pot. Darlene and Violet were right behind him, tugging sweatshirts over their pajamas to warm up.

"I think a snowstorm hit out there," Darlene said, her eyes peering out the frosted window. "Hey, is that a reindeer in the yard?"

There was no time to talk about Sweet William's new friends. Instead, Delia and Willow began speaking at the same time, creating their own blizzard of words as their explanations and excitement swirled this way and that.

The food pantry roof!

The hungry people who needed feeding!

The waffles!

Once Willow and Delia had finally caught their breath, Uncle Delvan poured his coffee and slowly turned to face them. He gazed at their faces with a thoughtful expression.

But it was Willow's big sister who finally broke the silence.

"We can make eggs," Violet volunteered. "Can't we, Darlene? We were really good cooks last summer when we almost worked for the café."

Willow rattled her head from side to side to make sure she was understanding them right. She'd expected to hear criticism from Violet and Darlene. Instead, their sisters were willing to help?

"Right," Darlene agreed. "Our food was fantastic! Do you remember, Dad?"

Uncle Delvan said he remembered their cooking *very well*. And Willow was relieved to see that he would be assisting the big sisters in their attempts at making breakfast. He pulled out a few frying pans and got right to work, showing Darlene and Violet how to crack eggs without getting shells in the bowl.

"Thanks," Delia began, clearly as stunned as Willow was. "You guys are great to help us out."

"Are you kidding?" Darlene said. "I've seen the way you are with the food pantry, Delia. This is a big deal."

"And we know how you are about Cat," added Violet, her eyes on Willow. "Plus, it's Christmas, so that trumps everything."

"And who knows," Darlene said with a smile, "Reverend Rickles might want us to sing and play our ukuleles!"

Willow wanted to fling her arms around their necks and hug them both. But with the whisk dripping waffle batter and the bowl heavy in her arms, she just gave both big sisters a grateful smile.

Aunt Deenie came in a few minutes later. And when she saw the assembly line forming in the café kitchen and heard the girls' story about the food pantry, she walked straight over to the cupboards where Cat stored the bulky items. She returned a few moments later lugging an enormous box of cocoa powder and a bag of white sugar.

"What we need is gallons and gallons of hot chocolate," she said. "I'll call over to Rosie and Aggie to come help. But if it's okay, girls, I'd like to keep this a secret from Cat and Mr. Henry. With this being their wedding day and all . . . well, you've taken on a tall order."

Cat! Willow had forgotten about her. Was she still upstairs, sound asleep? Willow felt like her tongue was tied in a knot. Thankfully, Delia was able to speak for the two of them.

"We can't let Cat see this kitchen!" she squeaked. "What if she knew we were getting ready to feed a hundred people over here? When we're supposed to be helping her get ready for the most important day of her whole life?"

Delia's mom and dad exchanged worried looks. Uncle Delvan said he'd keep watch on the staircase, just in case Cat made her way downstairs and toward the kitchen.

Before too long, as the waffles began to pile higher and higher on the plates and the eggs scrambled on the pans and the cocoa simmered in the deep pot, three more helpers arrived from Whispering Pines.

"What can we do?" asked Willow's mom, checklist in her hand and pencil at the ready.

"It's Jonathan's morning to handle the babies," said Aunt Rosie, picking up a long spoon and giving the cocoa a stir. "I can pitch in as long as you need me."

Aunt Deenie pointed toward the extra freezer in the back pantry and uttered one word: "Bacon!"

"We're on it!" called Willow's dad, grabbing Willow's mom by the hand and dashing down the hallway. "Come on, Aggie!"

Aunt Rosie pulled out another skillet and found some space at the stove beside the eggs. "Waffles, eggs, cocoa. And now bacon," she said, sniffing the heavenly aromas in the air. "What is breakfast without a little bacon?"

"What is *life* without a little bacon?" wondered Uncle Delvan.

Everything seemed to be going smoothly for those brief minutes. And Willow felt a rush of excitement for being able to help out—really do something important—for the food pantry with Delia.

But then the phone rang again.

The kitchen went silent. Even the hot cocoa seemed to stop its bubbling.

Willow could hear her heart pounding in her ears. Who was calling now? Reverend Rickles again? Was there something else wrong at the food pantry?

"Answer it," urged Delia, pushing Willow toward the phone.

"No way!" said Willow, pushing her cousin right back. "It's your house. You answer it!"

Delia gingerly picked up the receiver as Willow leaned her head in close. With all four of their hands eagerly clutching the phone, they pressed it to their ears.

"Hello?" whispered Delia.

But it wasn't Reverend Rickles on the line. This time, it was Cat!

"I could use y'all's help over here for a bit," she was saying. "I got up early enough to wake a rooster! Came over here to Whispering Pines to get things in order. I think we've got time to do one more dessert, maybe something with caramel, before the wedding. What do you girls think? Can I count on you?"

Willow stepped away from the phone, frantically shaking her head back and forth. *Noooo!* she was mouthing to Delia.

"Of course you can count on us," Delia told Cat. "We'll be right over!"

Once she'd hung up the phone, she turned to Willow. "What else could I say? It's her wedding day. And she needs our help!"

Willow stopped biting her knuckle. She took a deep breath to calm the butterflies in her stomach. Delia was right, today was Cat's big day. Tugging off their aprons, the two cousins slipped into their snow boots and raced across the wide white yard toward Whispering Pines.

Anything for Cat and her wedding.

"Y'all must be busy over there at Arts and Eats this mornin'," Cat was saying as they pulled out the sugar and the salt and set them on the island countertop in the middle of the kitchen. "You seem a little, well . . . flustered."

Willow stopped what she was doing and took a long look at Delia: her braids were a mess, a bit of eggshell was stuck on her elbow, and her forest-green junior bridesmaid dress was dusted in flour. Willow could see the exact border of where Delia's apron had ended; the rest of her skirt was a paler, flour-covered version of green. She looked down at her own skirt and saw the same thing!

"We're just getting ready for the big day is all," Willow said, pounding at her full skirt and trying to shake off the flour. She nudged Delia and pointed at her elbow. Delia flicked away the eggshell without Cat seeming to notice.

"Well, I thought we could whip up some caramel-coated nuts for this afternoon," Cat said. "I keep looking over at all those desserts we made this week, and I never feel like it's enough."

Willow forced a smile. And she saw Delia giving a stiff grimace as well. What if Cat discovered their secret? That there were only *half* as many desserts as Cat expected! And how could they stay here helping

Cat make another treat *and* finish the waffles for the food pantry? They'd have to get cracking and stirring and baking, fast!

"Sounds like a good idea," Willow said, hoping her voice sounded calm and cheerful. But inside her head, she wanted to shout, *There's no way we can do this! It's simply not possible!*

"Don't you think, Delia? A good idea?"

Her cousin was tugging on her braids with both hands. Willow wondered if one was going to come right off her head! "Yep, sounds great," Delia said, nearly hollering in her nervousness. "Just great!"

The cousins got busy toasting the pecans, almonds, cashews, and peanuts. They dumped sugar in another pan and drizzled water across the top. And before long they had a sweet-smelling caramel sauce to add to the nuts.

"You girls must really be excited to be my junior bridesmaids," Cat observed with a bit of wonder in her voice. "Because I've never seen y'all work so fast!"

"Very excited," Willow said, bouncing in her snow

boots. She had been in too much of a hurry to take them off. "In fact, we're so excited, we need to get our hair ready. Right, Delia? Yours is a mess!"

"Yours too!" said Delia, hollering for real this time as she flung the spatula onto the counter-top. "Your hair looks terrible! We've got to get a brush through it. Cat, we'll have to run back over to my house for a bit. Are you okay here?"

"Just call when you need us back!" added Willow, stumbling out the door with Delia on her heels. They didn't even give Cat a moment to respond.

And the *thwack!* of the screen door was the last they heard from the Whispering Pines kitchen as they raced back across the yard. Following the deep footprints they'd already left in the snow, their path led them toward the café's front door. And it kept them a safe distance from Sweet William's reindeer.

Chapter 19
dashing through the snow!

Both cousins had to raise their skirts to keep them from dragging in the snow as they dashed across the two yards. Willow heard a voice on the café's porch and looked up to see the carriage man from the other day talking with Grandma and Grandpa. His black horse stood patiently nearby, sending white puffs into the air with every breath.

"No, I don't think it's possible to send that carriage through the snow today," Grandma was saying. "But surely with your horse, there must be something we can do."

"By the looks of it, the only thing that can make

it through the snow is Santa's sleigh," joked Grandpa. "But I imagine the roads in town will be plowed in a few hours." *In a few hours?* Willow felt the butterflies in her stomach take flight. She and Delia didn't have a few hours. Cat's wedding started at noon. If they were going to feed Reverend Rickles's hungry families, it would have to happen soon!

Willow pulled Delia aside, near a porch pole that was decorated with wide red ribbon to look like a candy cane. The Arts & Eats Café still seemed cheerful despite all the tension around the waffle making.

"What can we do? We need something that can get through the snow to those food pantry families, but what?"

Delia smiled and pointed over Willow's shoulder into the yard. Then she ran to Grandma, Grandpa, and the carriage man at the front door.

"You're exactly right, Grandpa. Santa's sleigh can make it. And we've got one here!" she said, turning the group toward the bright red sleigh parked in the middle of the lawn. "My parents put it there as a Christmas decoration."

"But it's real," Willow added, her curls bouncing on her shoulders. "If we could hook the horse to that sleigh, we could bring lots of people over from the food pantry. That's how they did it in the old days! Right, Grandpa?"

"How old do you think I am?" exclaimed Grandpa, pretending to be offended. "I think that's a fine idea, girls." And turning to the carriage man, he added, "If your horse won't mind the deep snow, it's worth a try."

Once the garland was pulled off the sleigh and the rest of the decorations were moved onto the porch, the carriage driver began fiddling with the bars and straps. And before long, he tipped his hat toward Delia, Willow, Grandma, and Grandpa, and let out a hearty shout to his horse. The sleigh took off through the yard toward downtown, the bold red paint standing out against the white snow.

"Where's he going?" came a cry from the staircase

inside the house. The door was ajar, and Sweet William bounded outside onto the porch, binoculars dangling from his neck, cheeks flushed. "Stop that sleigh!"

"Where's *who* going, dear?" asked Grandma, looking all around.

"Santa Claus!" said Sweet William, practically shouting. "He's letting his reindeer rest out back. And now he's using a horse to pull his sleigh. Tricky move!"

He jumped off the porch and bounded into the yard. "I've got to catch Santa! I need to ask him something important."

Willow and Delia looked at each other, not sure what to say. Grandma and Grandpa were just as baffled.

"That man on the red sleigh wasn't—" Willow began, but Sweet William wouldn't be put off.

"Come on, Grandpa, we've got to catch him! Before it's too late!"

And Sweet William tried to run through the deep snow, his legs sinking up to his thighs with every step. Grandpa didn't seem to have the heart to set his grandson straight, so he grabbed his own hat and coat and followed quickly behind.

"If it's Santa Claus we're looking for," he called after Sweet William, "we need only believe. Then we'll find him."

Willow and Delia headed back into the café kitchen with Grandma at their side. They stepped right over to their mixing bowls, adding the flour and egg yolks and other ingredients to make more waffles. Violet and Darlene were still scrambling the eggs. And the three aunts stood in their bathrobes at a huge pot, stirring the hot cocoa like witches at a cauldron.

As she poured more batter for the waffles, Willow took a moment to look around. She was amazed at how much food was already cooked and waiting. Tall stacks of waffles towered on platters, scrambled eggs filled at least three long dishes, and crispy bacon perched in delicious-smelling mounds on plate after plate after plate.

"I don't know how many this will serve, but it's got to help," Willow said, stepping toward her dad and Uncle Delvan for hugs. "Thank you, everyone!"

"Yes," agreed Delia, her eyes looking a little wet with tears. "Thank you, everybody, for doing all this for the food pantry."

Willow was just putting a mug of cocoa to her lips when the phone rang again. And she knew right away who would be at the other end.

Cat.

"Hello?" said Delia, her eyes on Willow.

Willow watched as her cousin nervously gnawed on a clump of her hair. Cat needed them over at Whispering Pines again! But how would they be any help with the wedding preparation when they were thinking about the food pantry breakfast? And how could they be thinking about anything *but* Cat's wedding when it was only hours away? Willow's head was swimming!

"We've got to go back over," announced Delia once she'd hung up the phone.

"I know, I know," said Willow, her arms already in her coat. "Cat needs us again, and it's her special day. So let's get over there fast!"

"The faster we can help her," Delia said a little breathlessly as she raced toward the door, "the faster we can get back here before the food pantry families arrive!"

Jumping into their snow boots and again scooping up the hems of their skirts, the cousins dashed back across the yard to Whispering Pines. When they reached the kitchen, Cat was arranging platters of delicious-looking food—appetizers and sandwiches she'd prepared somehow during the busy week. She nodded toward the wide silver trays and asked the cousins to take them into the dining room.

Willow and Delia pushed through the swinging door, then stopped short, a little stunned. Cat's wedding cake stood at the center of the long table, a chocolate masterpiece in glittering silver sprinkles. Now it was crowned with a pair of chocolate-dipped pickles. Willow wasn't sure how good chocolatey pickles would taste, but she liked how they topped off the whole cake with style. And who knew? Cat and Mr. Henry might start a new food trend.

"Good morning, ladies," began Mr. Henry, with Cat stepping over to stand at his side. He wasn't wearing a hat today but kept reaching up to his head anyway as if to tip an invisible one. "Ms. Catherine and I could use your help assisting us with the desserts. We need them placed throughout the dining room and living room so guests may enjoy them to the fullest. Once you've settled the sandwich platters, would you mind lending us a hand with the cookies and treats?"

Willow and Delia sprang into action like a couple of windup toys, telling Mr. Henry and Cat that they could handle it themselves.

"No need for you to bother with desserts," Willow said, trying to block the way back into the kitchen with her body. She wanted to keep Mr. Henry and Cat from noticing anything unusual about the treats!

"We've got it all under control," Delia added, draping an arm over Willow's shoulder to keep the happy couple from slipping past. "You know you can count on us!"

Once Cat and Mr. Henry got busy with another task—rolling out a red carpet in the front room of Whispering Pines—the cousins shut the heavy door that led from the dining room into the kitchen. Opening all the containers, they began lining up the desserts on round plates, square plates, oval plates, silver plates, snowman-themed plates, anything they could find.

"Spread everything out wide so it looks like more food," Willow whispered. "Even with the extra peppermint bark, pretzels, and sugar cookies we made last night, there's so much still missing!"

"I'm trying," Delia hissed back. "If only we had those gingerbread loaves! I can't believe they're gone. What will Mr. Henry think when he finds out?"

Once the plates were ready, the cousins pushed back through the door and began covering the living and dining rooms with the sweet treats. They set desserts on tabletops, bookcases, the fireplace mantel, anywhere that had an inch of space. Cat stood in the center of things, and Willow could feel her eyes

studying them. Cat seemed to take in their dresses, their hair, and the dusting of breakfast ingredients that stuck everywhere. The snow boots probably didn't help either.

"You girls are looking like you're still, *ah* . . . getting yourselves ready," she said with a little hesitation in her voice.

It was obvious Delia and Willow weren't spending any time getting ready. They looked more like they'd been wrestling with Bernice than preparing themselves for a wedding.

Cat, however, looked gorgeous. She was wearing a white dress and a fitted white jacket. It was trimmed with a furry green collar that was the same shade as their junior bridesmaid dresses. She had a bright sprig of holly pinned to her jacket near her heart, and Willow was reminded of Mrs. Claus herself.

"You're beautiful, Cat," said Delia. "I've never seen you look so pretty!"

"She is a vision of loveliness, I agree," added Mr. Henry, and his cheeks burned almost as red as Cat's holly pin. "I am the luckiest man in the world."

Quickly enough, Willow and Delia finished arranging all the wedding desserts. They were ready to head back over to the Arts & Eats Café, knowing the hungry breakfast guests would be arriving any minute now. That is, so long as Reverend Rickles's truck could get through the snow and the red sleigh had reached the food pantry.

"Tell that little brother of yours to come over with Bernice for a practice run," Cat said as the cousins opened the door onto the porch. "And your sisters, too. We need to hear them perform the wedding march so we know how fast or slow to walk down the aisle. Send them all over, if you don't mind!"

Delia and Willow promised they would and started back for the café.

"And don't forget to get yourselves, *ah . . .*" Cat hollered, a long pause hanging in the air. ". . . lookin' like junior bridesmaids!"

Chapter 20
uh-oh!

Willow and Delia were back in the café kitchen in a flash, their bodies trembling. And it wasn't from the freezing temperatures and the waist-high snowdrifts. The cousins were eager to get the food pantry breakfast going.

They had just dusted off layers of snowflakes from their green gowns when Violet and Darlene stepped in. Their big sisters were dressed for Cat's wedding in matching red velvet dresses. And Violet was carrying their ukuleles.

"Violet and Darlene, you should go over to Cat and Mr. Henry now," directed Willow. She looked like a commander ready for battle, a long piece of bacon in one hand like a pointer and one of her mom's pencils in the other. "Keep them occupied at Whispering Pines while the food pantry's guests arrive here for the waffle breakfast."

Willow flipped over a recipe card and began writing down her own checklist, just the way her mom always did. She began ticking things off as she and Delia spoke.

"The rest of you," ordered Delia, her library monitor voice loud and clear, "Aunt Aggie, Grandma, Aunt Rosie, Mom—you finish getting yourselves dressed and ready for the wedding. The triplets need . . ."

Suddenly, Delia froze. The triplets! Willow wondered what would happen to her and Delia if they had to juggle June, July, and August along with everything else?

"We'll take the little angels," announced Uncle Delvan. "Liam and I can help Jonathan get them dressed and clean."

Willow and Delia heaved sighs of relief. "Just keep

them away from orange goop," Delia whispered, giving Willow's shoulder a quick nudge.

"And take away their spoons," added Willow quietly, nudging her right back.

Willow's mom nodded her approval, not only of the fathers handling the triplets but of Willow's organization skills too. She even tugged another pencil from her hair and passed it to Willow, along with one of her notebooks. Willow gave her a grateful smile.

Aunt Deenie was all business.

"Willow and Delia, I hope you'll stay put in the kitchen and finish preparing the last of the breakfast. When Aggie and I come downstairs"—she reached out her hands to touch Delia's crazy braids and Willow's even crazier curls—"we'll deal with your hair."

Quick as butter melting on a hot skillet, everyone disappeared, leaving Willow and Delia alone in the kitchen. The girls poured the last of the batter into the waffle irons and closed the lids, then turned to face each other. Willow took a deep breath, inhaling the comforting smells of vanilla, hot cocoa, and warm waffles.

"Just think about it, Delia! This might be the best Christmas morning we ever have in our whole lives."

Delia agreed. "Even though it's been hard running back and forth between the houses, I think we're doing good. We're helping people who need it, and we're helping Cat. And so far, we've got it all under control!"

"Exactly," Willow whispered, almost too afraid to say it out loud in case it jinxed them. "We don't have lucky pennies or lucky hummingbirds, or even good-luck threes. But we've got Christmas magic!"

"That's right!" grinned Delia. "With Christmas magic, what could possibly go wrong?"

They were about to find out.

"Girls, where's Sweet William?"

Willow's mom was back in the kitchen now and wearing her fancy dress for the wedding. She'd had time to change out of her bathrobe, but her hair was in enormous curlers.

"He went out with Grandpa a while back, Aunt Aggie," Delia explained. "They were in search of Santa Claus, I think."

"Oh, good heavens!" gasped Willow's mom. And pointing over their shoulders toward the kitchen window, she exclaimed, "It looks like he found him!"

Delia and Willow raced to the window and pressed their faces close to the cold glass. The red sleigh had just pulled up in front of Whispering Pines. A jolly looking man wearing a bright red suit was helping people up the stairs.

And right behind the red sleigh was a big blue truck with a giant shovel attached to the front.

"That's a snowplow!" shouted Willow. "And look! Grandpa and Sweet William are in the front seat beside the driver."

Delia shook her head in disbelief. She rubbed at the glass to clear the moisture that had built up. "The snowplow must have opened the road for all the drivers," she said, trying to make sense of what they were seeing. "Willow, look over there! Do you see all those cars pulling into the driveway?"

Another few seconds passed as they watched the curious scene across the way. Then it seemed to hit them all at the same time.

"That's Reverend Rickles in the Santa suit!" shouted Delia.

"Those aren't guests for Cat's wedding. They're the families for the food pantry breakfast! They're at the wrong house!"

Willow's mom pressed her face against the glass now too. "Cat is probably passed out on the floor from having so many strangers show up in her living room! She was expecting our family for the wedding, not the whole town!"

Yanking the curlers from her hair, she yelled, "Girls, we've got to move it!"

And at the same time, Willow and Delia both shouted, "Run!"

They took off across the hardwood floors for the front door. Willow's mom grabbed her snow boots and hollered to her sisters and mother about the latest twist in their morning.

Delia and Willow pulled on their coats for the third—or was it fourth? Willow had lost count!— time that morning. Aunt Deenie, Aunt Rosie, and Grandma were downstairs in a flash too, joining them in the mad dash through the snow to Whispering Pines.

But by the time they reached the old white Victorian and climbed the porch steps, the cat was out of the bag.

In more ways than one.

Tabitha, the orange tabby cat who had adopted the food pantry, was sitting on the red sleigh and mewing for someone to carry her over the snow and inside the warm house. Willow swept Tabby up in her arms and introduced her to Bernice and Gossie, who were curious but welcoming. Tabby was too tubby to bother with any of them, and she wandered into the house, probably to find a good place to nap. Bill, Pat, and Jimmy honked and waddled after her.

Willow's knees were shaking as she stepped through the front door into Whispering Pines beside Delia. What was Cat going to say? How could they possibly explain why so many strangers had just arrived in the living room? Especially when a wedding was only hours away?

The cousins timidly shuffled into the foyer. Cat and Mr. Henry were nearby, talking with the man who was dressed up in the red suit like Santa Claus. And when he turned, Willow recognized him right away. Delia had been right—it really was Reverend Rickles.

"Good morning, Miss Delia, Miss Willow," said Mr. Henry with a polite bow. "My brother was just explaining to me the distressing situation with the food pantry and its former roof—"

"We're so sorry!" interrupted Willow. "We didn't want anyone going hungry—"

"We only meant to help!" added Delia, who interrupted Willow's interruption. "It's Christmas, after all!"

And in one swift motion, Cat stepped over and stood directly in front of both cousins. She seemed as if she might cry.

Willow took one look at Cat's expression, and a wave of regret washed over her. "We didn't mean to turn your wedding day into another disaster," she croaked, fighting back tears.

"We really did want to do the right thing," Delia added, her voice a whisper. "But sometimes it's confusing—what's the *rightest* right thing to do."

Cat looked hard into their faces, her cat's-eye glasses framing her eyes as she pressed in close.

Willow gulped. Delia tugged on her braids. It was clear to Willow that Cat was really going to let them have it, so before Cat could say a word, Willow decided to try to make things right.

"Delia and I want to explain everything," she began, having to pause for a bit of nervous gulping. "But it's easier to let you see for yourself."

And they turned Cat around to face the dining room, where a fresh table had just been set up. The aroma of warm waffles filled the air as Willow's dad, Uncle Delvan, and Uncle Jonathan pulled off the covers of all the breakfast platters and pots they'd carried over from the Arts & Eats Café. Grandpa was seated nearby, somehow balancing three squirming babies on his lap.

"Breakfast for a hundred," said Delia, tugging nervously on her braids again, "We wanted to do something special for your wedding, like a fancy dinner or an amazing dessert. . . ."

Mr. Henry stepped over and picked up a small

strip of bacon. Turning to Cat and the cousins, he began to nibble.

"There are many Christmas stories of the three wise men of olden days," he said, "bringing gold, frankincense, and myrrh. But it looks like today we have three wise fellows delivering us eggs, bacon, and hot cocoa."

Willow could barely bring her eyes to meet Cat's. What was she going to say? Looking around the crowded room, it was hardly the picture-perfect wedding Cat had hoped for. Willow and Delia might as well confess about the missing desserts, too.

Willow squeezed her eyes shut, dreading this moment.

"You girls . . ." Cat began, her words hanging in the air.

Willow opened one eye, peeking over at Delia.

"You girls . . ." Cat said again, catching her breath. "You have given us the best wedding present we could ever imagine. The best!"

And in Cat's Southern way of talking, it came out sounding like *bay-est*.

Raising her hands above her head, Cat spun slowly around to encompass the entire downstairs in the sweep of her arms. Families from the food pantry were everywhere, seated in folding chairs for the wedding, clustered around the fireplace, gathered near the wedding cake. Violet and Darlene were playing Christmas carols on their ukuleles, and a handful of volunteers in their bright red sweatshirts were singing too.

Mrs. Rudolph was at the center of them, belting out the chorus louder than anyone else. She waved over to Delia and Willow. The cousins gave nervous waves back.

"Henry and I were just talking with his brother," Cat continued. "There's just the two of us, you know: no children or grandchildren of our own. We have y'all, of course, and your wonderful family. But this? We never dreamed we'd have so many people take part in our celebration."

Cat's face was beaming as she spun around again, taking in the whole house.

"This sure beats all! Today's wedding is our chance to share what we can," Cat said, scooping a waffle onto a plate and passing it to a boy walking past. "You've given us something pretty amazing, girls. I'm happier than a partridge in a pear tree, y'all!"

a wedding, with a hundred surprise guests

Willow and Delia flung themselves into Cat's arms. And they stood there in a merry group hug as the Christmas carols played. Willow was too happy and relieved to worry about blocking the path to the dining room. But when she saw her mom and aunts pushing past, their arms loaded down with cardboard crates and food boxes, she and Delia finally let go.

The cousins stepped over to help, each taking a crate from their moms. But as the box flaps popped open, Willow's sense of holiday cheer quickly transformed into something very different.

"Hey, what is this?" she shouted, fumbling with

the flaps and peering inside. "There are cookies in here! Cookies that we made in Cat's kitchen. Delia, look! I've found our missing desserts!"

Delia peeked into her box too and pulled out the same thing—the missing snowball cookies, the vanishing peppermint bark, the disappearing chocolate-dipped pretzels with rainbow sprinkles. "And the Rickles family's favorite! Gingerbread—both containers!"

"I beg your pardon, ladies," began Mr. Henry, reaching up and forgetting again that he wasn't wearing a hat. "Perhaps I neglected to inform you of the arrangement we worked out with my brother. It involves the food pantry."

Both girls looked over at Reverend Rickles, their eyebrows raised.

"That's right, girls," he said, adjusting the black belt on his Santa suit. "Have you not heard about our volunteer committee? We've been collecting donations from restaurants and kitchens around town this whole week. I picked up a few items from Cat's kitchen, even last night—hope I didn't wake you. You see, we're sending families home with boxes of food for the holidays."

Willow nudged Delia with her shoulder.

And Delia nudged her right back.

"Does this volunteer committee have a name?" asked Delia, her eyes twinkling with laughter.

"You haven't heard of us already?" wondered Reverend Rickles. "We're called Santa's Elves. I thought you saw the sign-up sheet at the food pantry. No?"

Willow burst out laughing, the box of desserts bouncing in her arms. "Santa's Elves! Of course! Everyone told us that!"

"But we thought they meant, you know," Delia began, "the *real* Santa's elves. . . ."

Suddenly, Sweet William was beside them, tugging on Reverend Rickles's red sleeve. He looked a little nervous as he turned his face up to the reverend. And Willow realized that her brother had a sincere request to make.

"I know you might just be a substitute Santa," Sweet William began, his voice a whisper. "But there's something very important I've got to ask you for."

Reverend Rickles leaned in closer. So Willow and Delia did too.

"Go ahead, son, tell me what it is," Reverend Rickles encouraged.

And Sweet William stretched on his tiptoes, cupping both his hands around his mouth and whispering into Reverend Rickles's ear.

"Oh, son, that's a wonderful Christmas wish. But I think my brother and Cat already *are* living happily ever after," he whispered back. "The real Santa would be very impressed with you."

Mr. Henry and Cat beamed at each other, clearly ready to exchange their vows. They stepped into the living room and called the wedding ceremony to order now that all the food pantry families and other guests had arrived. Willow and Delia took their positions at the far end of the room, near the front door. They were ready to walk down the red-carpeted aisle as junior brides-maids. But suddenly a commotion in the coat closet drew away everyone's attention.

"Where did that orange cat come from?" some-one asked.

"There isn't just one cat in there," said someone else. "There are five!"

"Good gravy!" came another voice, and Willow knew right away that it belonged to Reverend Rickles. "Tabitha delivered kittens!"

His eyes were bright as he emerged from the hanging coats and found his brother. He held a tiny calico ball of fur in his hands. "What do you know, Henry? Kittens on your wedding day. A bride named Cat. I think this was destiny."

Cat and Mr. Henry stood there stunned, like a

couple of ice sculptures. Their eyes were wide and their jaws hung open. After a few silent moments—interrupted only by a happy woof from Bernice and a few honks from Gossie's family—Cat was able to speak.

"Well, Henry, I think we'll have to keep them. That is, if Tabitha doesn't mind calling Whispering Pines home. After all, when there's a Cat around, there should be a kitten or two!"

And this made the whole room erupt with laughter. Now everybody, including Reverend Rickles, headed toward the living room again to try for a second time to get the wedding started. Guests and families took their seats in the white folding chairs on both sides of the red carpet. And Violet and Darlene picked up their ukuleles to begin the wedding march.

They'd just begun strumming when the ceremony was interrupted again. Only it wasn't the high-pitched yowl of a mama cat delivering kittens. It was deeper than that, and it was coming from the yard between Whispering Pines and the Arts & Eats Café.

"*Ho ho ho!* Merry Christmas! *Ho ho ho!*"

Willow heard it and whipped her head toward Delia. Delia raised a single eyebrow in response. Who could be out there in the yard making such a racket?

"Santa Claus!" screeched Sweet William. And he raced to the window, Willow and Delia at his side. Their eyes scanned the yard for any sign of a red sleigh or a jolly man with a long white beard.

"Dasher and Dancer! They're gone!" shouted Sweet William. "Santa must have decided it was time to go. So he took all the reindeer!"

"Elk!" corrected Delia.

But when she looked down at Sweet William's expression, she softened a bit. "I mean *elf*, not elk. I . . . *ummm* . . . I thought I saw an elf behind that tree."

Willow gave Delia an enormous grin. And they put their hands on Sweet William's shoulders and gently turned him around to join the rest of the wedding party at their proper places. With the desserts laid out beside the steaming waffle-eggs-and-bacon breakfast, the spirit of holiday cheer was swirling in the air. Now the guests turned their attention for the third time to the wedding ceremony.

Violet and Darlene strummed their ukuleles, playing a peppy version of the wedding march. First down the aisle paraded the triplets, who carried out their jobs as flower babies with help from the three aunts.

Willow and Delia were next, looping arms and marching down the red carpet in a fit of giggles. Never in the history of junior bridesmaids had there been such an excited pair. And even though their dresses were decorated with spots of white flour, their snow boots sounded clunky under their velvet skirts, their wrists and elbows were freckled with bits of waffle batter and eggshells, and their hair could have used a few hours of proper attention, they did a fantastic job.

Sweet William was all smiles as he stood beside Mr. Henry and Reverend Rickles in his role as best boy. And when the time came to hand over the wedding rings, he only had to look in four pockets before he found them, safe and sound.

Once the vows and the kisses were exchanged, Whispering Pines erupted in clapping and shouts and whistles, which quickly turned into Christmas carols about love and joy and winter wonderlands.

"Before we start with the Christmas feast," began Mr. Henry, again reaching for his hat and forgetting it wasn't there, "I'd like to say thanks to two special young ladies, Delia Dees and Willow Sweeney. They've reminded all of us of the magic of Christmas. And for Cat and myself, well, they've given us a real gift: love and joy."

Willow and Delia threw their arms around each other, bouncing and hooting and barely able to contain themselves. They were a churning stew of emotions: embarrassment for being singled out, happiness for Cat and Mr. Henry finally tying the knot, and sheer delight at seeing all their food on plates and platters and tabletops around the house.

"That's right!" declared Willow, turning to Delia in delight. "Love and joy—and waffles!"

Chapter 22
a happy new year

It was almost a week later when Cat and Mr. Henry returned from their honeymoon.

"We were just like those hummingbirds, y'all," Cat said with a laugh. "We flew all the way to Mexico for sunshine and warm weather. It felt great to be there, but it feels even better to be back—even though there's still three feet of snow everywhere."

The whole family was hunkered down in the Arts & Eats Café as another blizzard raged outside, the wind whipping at the windows and howling through the closed doors. The hot cocoa tasted extra delicious to Willow, who wiggled her toes in her warm wool socks as she watched the snowflakes swirl across the yard. Delia snuggled closer in the chair they were sharing. When no one was looking, she slipped more marshmallows into their mugs.

"Let's hear about honeymoon adventures," encouraged Aunt Deenie. "After all the excitement of your wedding ceremony, we want more!"

But Mr. Henry said the honeymoon was quiet— free from surprise visits by one hundred hungry guests, newborn kittens, or jolly holiday celebrities.

"We're glad you're back in time for our New Year's tradition," Grandma said, setting down her cocoa mug. And she began to explain what the whole family was doing.

"We have a jar here." She held up a clear glass jar with a shiny silver lid. "In it, we slip a note that says our name and a resolution for the coming year. Then when the next New Year's

Eve rolls around, we pull out the slips and see whether we've met our goals or not."

Grandpa said New Year's resolutions reminded him of his favorite flowers, little blue forget-me-nots. "I write down what I want to do on this paper, then I spend the whole year trying not to forget what it was!"

As last year's papers tumbled out of the jar and onto the table, Violet and Darlene gave each other pats on the back. They had promised to try something new, and they'd done that a few times over. They'd both learned to play the ukulele. They'd formed a band—the Umbrellas. And they'd tried to get good at cooking, though Willow wouldn't exactly call them successful.

"I met my goal," Delia announced. "I had written down 'do something useful.' And I think working at the food pantry is useful. It's *helpful*, at least. Right?"

"It's not just useful and helpful," said Cat, "it's downright wonderful. Makes me want to join you, Delia."

Delia told Cat she could come along with her and Reverend Rickles anytime.

Uncle Jonathan and Aunt Rosie had written down the same goals for the past year: their papers both read "sleep." And for the coming year, they agreed that the triplets shared the same resolution: "learn how to walk!"

Grandma wrinkled her nose when she read her goal from last year. "I wanted to learn to dance the tango. But with this old hollyhock staying rooted like he is . . ." And she swiped at Grandpa's arm.

"Old hollyhock?" he demanded. "Shall I remind you what the tree once said when he was bothered? *Leaf* me alone!"

Grandpa said his goal had been to spend more time with the family. "And with our trips here, I believe I have. I've enjoyed every minute."

After everyone else had taken a turn, only Sweet William and Willow were left to share their resolutions.

"Mine was to catch Santa's reindeer so I could talk

to him in person," Sweet William said, holding up his slip of paper and showing the whole family.

And with his other hand, he was holding something else. He slowly opened his fingers to reveal what was resting on his palm. A tooth!

"I lost it when I bit into my breakfast," he said, holding it up for everyone to see. "So I've decided that for this coming year, my goal will be to catch the Tooth Fairy! There are a few things I need to ask her."

Willow was the last to go. She finished writing her resolution for the new year and folded the paper tight. Dropping it into the jar, she picked up the silver lid and sealed all the papers inside until next New Year's Eve.

"Last year's goal was to learn how to make an upside-down cake, which I did back in April," she said, trying not to sound boastful. "It wasn't all that hard."

But she didn't want to share what she'd written

for the coming year. That was too much like sharing birthday wishes: if you told, they wouldn't come true. So she kept quiet, sneaking a peek at Delia and smiling.

Delia smiled right back.

"We can make it happen," Delia whispered. "We'll find a way to get you here in Saugatuck! For longer than just a week or two!"

Willow's mouth dropped open in surprise, and her eyes darted to the jar of New Year's resolutions. "How did you know what I wrote?"

It was those amber eyes again. They saw things the same way.

"We can hear you girls," said Willow's dad, who was staring at the glass jar and the papers inside. "And we don't want to disappoint anybody, but we won't be moving away from Chicago anytime soon."

And now his gaze was on Willow.

"*Special* means something that is different from the usual. And what makes our time together here at

Whispering Pines and the yellow house so *special* is that it doesn't happen every day. That's why we treasure it."

Willow felt a lump in her throat. She wasn't going to let herself cry. But still. The new year was only hours away, and already her resolution was failing. How could this be?

"And leaving Chicago wouldn't make anyone's troubles disappear," added Willow's mom.

"But Willow faced them," said Violet. "When she and Delia did all that stuff for the food pantry and the wedding, all of it—Willow proved herself. That's a big deal, Mom."

Now Willow's eyes really were wet. She blinked as fast as she could to keep the tears from falling. She wanted to thank Violet for taking her side, but she didn't think the words would come.

"We're proud of you, Willow," said her mom. "And while we're not ready to move here like you want, Dad and I understand that you really, *really* love being in Saugatuck."

"So we've spoken with Delvan and Deenie," continued her dad, "and we were thinking that if it's all right with Delia and you, well . . ." And he paused a beat or two. "When school lets out, we'd like to send you here to stay for the whole summer vacation."

The whole summer?

Willow and Delia didn't even have to answer. They swept out of their chairs, slipping and spinning and skating in their thick socks around the table in a noisy swirl of joy. They didn't tumble onto the floor like they usually did on the lawn in the summertime. But their whoops and cheers and laughter seemed to rattle the windows and shake the floors—even more than the blizzard outside.

It was enough to let their parents know that they liked the idea.

"You girls are like a couple of snowballs," said Uncle Delvan. "Getting bigger and bigger with every turn!"

Suddenly, Willow and Delia stopped their celebrating and stared into each other's faces.

"Snowballs!" exclaimed Willow with a bounce.

"I almost forgot!" hollered Delia, her face full of the same fizzy excitement.

And the cousins raced into the Arts & Eats Café's kitchen and returned with a long platter balanced between them.

"We wanted to celebrate Cat and Mr. Henry's return," began Delia.

"And New Year's Eve," added Willow with a shout.

"Along with the crazy blizzard!"

"And the whole family being together!"

"And the new kittens, Lucky, Penny, Birdy, and Magic!"

"And—"

"All right, all right!" hollered Violet and Darlene, who were clearly losing patience. "We get it. *Celebrating*. But what's on the tray?"

The cousins set the platter in the center of the table, beaming with pride as they draped an arm around the other's shoulder.

"They're snowballs," said Willow, her bright curls tangling together with Delia's black braids.

"Snowball *cupcakes*," Delia added, her eyes bright. "We decided to stop trying to make all the fancy dishes and get back to what we do best."

And at the same moment, Willow and Delia and every single member of the Bumpus family—including the honorary ones—seated around the long table uttered the exact same word:

"Cupcakes!"

Willow & Delia's Winter Wonders Snowball Cupcakes

Ingredients:
½ cup (1 stick) butter, softened
1 cup sugar
5 large egg whites
2 teaspoons vanilla extract
2 cups all-purpose flour
2 teaspoons baking powder
¼ teaspoon salt
¾ cup milk

Frosting ingredients:
1 cup (2 sticks) butter, softened
1 cup powdered sugar
½ teaspoon vanilla
1 7.5 ounce jar marshmallow creme
2 cups shredded coconut

Directions:

1. Make sure you have an adult's help.

2. Heat the oven to 350 degrees. Line muffin tins with liners.

3. Using an electric mixer, cream butter and sugar together until smooth. Add egg whites and mix well.

4. Add vanilla.

5. In a separate bowl, mix flour, baking powder, and salt.

6. Slowly combine the flour mixture into the creamy mixture. Blend in the milk. Mix well.

7. Pour batter into lined cupcake cups.

8. Bake for 18–20 minutes, or until toothpick inserted into cupcakes comes out clean.

9. Let cool completely before frosting.

10. Frosting: Place butter in a mixing bowl, and using an electric mixer, blend until creamy.

11. Slowly add powdered sugar, by quarter-cup scoops.

12. Add vanilla. Mix well.

13. Add in the marshmallow creme until frosting is fluffy and delicious. But do not overmix!

Making the snowballs:

1. Once the cupcakes have cooled completely, layer on the frosting.

2. Pour the shredded coconut into a bowl.

3. Holding the cupcakes by the base, dip the frosted tops into the bowl of coconut.

4. Your snowballs are ready to eat and enjoy! And bonus: you don't have to keep them in the freezer!

Makes about 20 cupcakes.

BEACH

ARTS
& EATS
CAFE

BLUE BERRY
BUSHES